Beneath the Surface

Danger in Destiny
Book 3

Melanie D. Snitker

DALLIONE MEDIA, LLC

Beneath the Surface
Danger in Destiny: Book 3
By Melanie D. Snitker

Dallionz Media, LLC
P.O. Box 5283
Abilene, TX 79608

Cover Art: Dallionz Media, LLC

Melanie D. Snitker
melanie@melaniedsnitker.com
www.melaniedsnitker.com

This is a work of fiction. Names, characters, businesses, places, events, and incidents either are the products of the author's imagination or used in a fictitious manner. Any resemblance to actual persons, living or dead, or actual events is purely coincidental.

In loving memory of
James C. Snitker
June 24, 1957 – August 24, 2023
Forever loved and missed.

Chapter One

D r. Genevieve "Eve" Marks put her phone on speaker and set it on top of the counter. Her mother's voice filled the small bathroom as Eve reached for her hairbrush.

"The spa is incredible, Genevieve. I've already gone three times this week. I told your dad that I'm going to have to find a place like this once we get back home." Noises in the background punctuated Mom's words. "The mud bath. I never thought I'd enjoy sitting in a tub full of mud, but it's done wonders for my skin."

Eve stifled a chuckle and ran the brush through her red hair, static electricity pulling at several strands and making them stretch from her head to the brush. "I'm glad you're having fun, Mom."

Her parents loved to travel, but this year, they decided to take their first cruise to celebrate their forty-fifth anniversary. They were somewhere in the Bahamas for two weeks, and Eve had a feeling this was going to be the start of a yearly ritual for them.

"What about you, Dad?" Eve spoke loudly, knowing her

parents had the phone on speaker. "What's been your favorite part of the cruise so far?"

"Besides spending time with your mom?" His comment was followed by Mom's "Awwww!" and the sound of them kissing. "The food, my girl. The food here is amazing. We should always have buffets available. There was even a taco bar last night."

Eve laughed out loud. She could picture Dad standing in line at the taco bar and piling his plate high. She also had no doubt he'd complained about heartburn later that night.

After scooping her hair into a high ponytail, she secured it with a band and tightened it in place. A quick glance at the mirror assured her she was ready to leave for work.

"Maybe next year you can come with us," Mom said.

"Oh, I wouldn't want to be a third wheel. And I love that you guys have these adventures together."

As far as Eve was concerned, her parents' relationship was an example of what a marriage should be like. They had so much fun together and were as much best friends as they were husband and wife. Eve could only hope that she would find that herself one day.

Dad's voice came over the line. Noise that sounded like dishes clinked in the background. "Your mother has been telling everyone that'll listen about the newspaper article."

Eve groaned. "Oh, Mom. No one there knows me. I'm sure they have other things they'd rather talk about." A particularly difficult case last month was solved thanks in part to the autopsy she performed on the victim. The local newspaper caught wind of the story and ran an article focused on her. Honestly, it was way more attention than she preferred.

Her mom had framed multiple copies of it and spread

the word in Clearwater until everyone in her parents' small town knew all about it.

"Nonsense. Is it so bad that your proud mother likes to share your achievement?"

The background noises were getting louder. Eve suspected they were entering the dining area.

"No. It's not so bad. Guys, I hate to cut you off, but I need to get in to work."

"We understand, honey." Mom raised her voice above the din.

"You guys go have fun. Try to behave yourselves."

"I promise nothing," Dad said with a laugh. "You be safe, sweetie. We'll call you again tomorrow."

"Love you, Genevieve."

"I love you both, too. Bye."

Eve hung up, put her phone in her bag, and slung it over her shoulder. Thankfully, where her parents' town might be fixated on the article that highlighted her accomplishments, Destiny, Texas didn't seem to be quite as focused. There were a few people who made mention of it, but most of them knew her beforehand. Her work as a medical examiner was somewhat old news, which was just fine with her.

She exited the small house she rented, locked the door behind her, and got into her navy-blue Jeep Compass. She lived across town from the Destiny Police Department, where she worked in the morgue as the only medical examiner in the county. This job might not pay as much as an ME in a larger city, but Eve wouldn't trade it for anything. She got to do the job she loved—bringing answers and closure for victims and their families—while living just over an hour away from her parents.

Once at the precinct, she parked and made a beeline for the break room. Coffee was an absolute must. Tia from dispatch made it every morning, and it rivaled the best coffee shops in town. Eve once asked Tia where she bought the coffee, but she wouldn't reveal her source. It was too bad because Eve would love to be able to brew a cup on her days off.

The heavenly smell greeted her when she walked into the break room, quickly followed by the almost equally tantalizing aroma of Detective John Paris's cologne. He'd just poured himself a cup and lifted the coffee pot. "Care for some?"

Eve snatched a to-go cup and held it out. "Please."

He filled it for her with a smile. The same amazing smile that had many of the single women who worked in the building whispering about the handsome, single detective behind his back.

Not Eve, though. Oh, she agreed he was attractive, with incredibly kind brown eyes and a willingness to help anyone. But she wasn't in the business of acting like a teenager gossiping about the cute boy in class.

"The weekend went by way too fast," he said conversationally. The blue button-down shirt he wore fit him like a glove.

"It sure did." Eve placed a lid on her cup and took a grateful sip. "My parents are on a cruise in the Bahamas. While cruises don't really appeal to me, I can't help but be a little jealous of their warm weather. I'm ready for summer."

"I'll remind you that you said that when it's a hundred and ten out."

Eve chuckled. "Yeah, you do that."

She was about to take another sip when Carl from the mailroom ducked his head around the doorframe.

"Oh, good. I thought I saw you walk by and was hoping I'd catch you." Carl entered the break room with a small box in his hands. "This just came in for you, Eve." He handed it to her.

The box reminded Eve of the type that held a coffee mug. She'd half expected it to have the weight of one as well but was surprised when it felt like there was nothing in it at all. "Thanks, Carl."

He smiled and left the room.

"Expecting something?" John asked.

"No." Eve gently shook it, but nothing moved around inside. There was no return address, and most of the space was covered in stamps. On the front, Dr. Genevieve Marks and the precinct address were typed onto a piece of paper. She turned it around to show John. "A little weird, right?"

"Yeah." He set his coffee down on the small table and stepped closer. "You don't usually get personal mail here?"

"This is a first." Most deliveries she got pertained to the morgue, arrived in bulk, and were delivered to the large doors in the back. "Let's see what's in here."

She put her coffee cup down and withdrew a large pocketknife that she used to slice through the tape. The flap was tucked inside, and it took a little maneuvering to get it to slide up and out.

With the box in one hand, she used the other to remove the tissue paper on top, revealing a large, black rose. Memories and emotions she'd spent years locking away tried to push their way in like a tidal wave. It took everything in Eve not to drop the box, but her hands shook with the effort.

"Eve?" A head taller than Eve, John had to lean down to look at her face. "What is it?"

She said nothing as she carefully set the box down on the table. Then she withdrew a pair of latex gloves from one of her pockets. When she pulled them on, John wordlessly stepped into action.

He moved in closer, her shoulder brushing up against his arm. He used his phone to take several pictures of the box, both the outside and the contents, and then nodded for her to continue.

If there was one thing her job had taught her, it was how to compartmentalize. She put those skills to use and shoved her own emotions into the closet where she'd deal with them later.

There was something beneath the flower. Eve carefully withdrew the rose, pulled the slightly bent envelope from the bottom, and set the flower back down. This was one of those fancy envelopes. The kind that you'd expect to contain a wedding invitation or something similar.

She turned it over, taking in the gold trim that outlined the sealed flap. She carefully ran a finger beneath the flap and lifted it. The first thing she saw was the dreaded newspaper article she'd been featured in. Next, she slid a piece of cardstock out of the envelope.

Given the fancy paper, she didn't expect to find the words on the card typed in a basic font that wasn't the least bit elegant.

Eve gasped as she read,

"Nice article. But soon they'll see the truth. The great Genevieve Marks will fall just like the rest of them."

Chill bumps raced up her arms.

The message made no sense. Fall how? With the article included, she thought it must refer to her job. But then, if someone had an issue with her, why not come to her directly?

A light touch to her elbow made her jump. She'd nearly forgotten John was there with her. He was standing close enough to read the note. "Have you received anything like this before?"

"No." She stared at the note another second or two, then slid it back into the envelope. She tucked it in beside the rose.

"Do you have a spare glove?"

Eve opened the bag she still had slung over her shoulder and handed him a pair.

John put them on. "I'll take it to the lab. Have them process it for fingerprints and anything else they can find." He seemed to wait for her agreement. When she nodded, he scooped the box up. "I'll be right back."

Eve took in a steadying breath. Then another.

As soon as John left the box and its contents with the lab, he jogged back to the break room. Eve was still there, her gaze fixed on a spot on the floor. When he entered, her chin lifted.

"Thank you for taking it. Did they say when they thought they'd have the results?"

"They didn't, but I requested that they send both of us a copy as soon as they have them."

Whoever sent this clearly knew the black rose would make an impact. He didn't think he'd ever forget the way the color had drained from her face when she saw it.

"What was it about the flower?"

She stared at something behind him, as though looking into the past, before her focus snapped back to his face. "There was a black rose in a case years ago..." Her voice trailed off, and her green eyes filled with pain.

He wanted her to elaborate. Whatever had happened with the other case clearly had a lasting effect on her. Had she been part of the investigation? Or was she a witness?

Before he had a chance to ask, Chief of Police Arnold Dolman slapped the doorframe. "We've got a dead body at the Gale Apartments. I need you both to head that way. Durant says it's the manager, and the tenants are causing a scene."

He paused just long enough for John to say, "Right away, sir." John picked up his cup of coffee and turned to Eve. "Are you going to be okay?"

"Yep." She retrieved her own coffee. "I'll meet you there." With a last smile that didn't quite reach her eyes, she left the break room.

He had every intention of asking for more details later. If someone were stalking Eve or threatening her in any way, John would make sure to find the person responsible. In the five years that he'd known Eve since transferring to the Destiny Police Department, and he'd never known her to be anything but kind, competent, and dependable. And he'd seen her work on a variety of cases that would bother anyone.

He never thought someone would have the ability to throw her off balance like the package did this morning.

Five minutes later, he maneuvered his car around a news van and parked near an impressive crowd of people that had gathered outside of an old, four-story apartment building. This wasn't the best part of Destiny, and the building fit right in. It badly needed fresh paint and repaired sidewalks, and John counted at least four broken windows. Plywood had been nailed in place, which was against code since the windows could no longer be used to escape the building in case of a fire.

As he got out of his car, a portly reporter named Al Crispin exited the news van and bustled toward him. "Excuse me. Can you comment on the scene? Is it true someone has been found dead inside?" The reporter nearly tripped over his own feet in his haste to lessen the distance between them.

Obviously, the reporter knew who John was by sight because there were no markings on his car to identify him otherwise. Even still, couldn't he see that John had just gotten there? How could he possibly have answers for anyone yet? "This is a developing case. A statement will be issued once we know more about the situation."

He ignored the other questions that followed as he spotted Eve's Compass pulling into the parking lot. He didn't want Crispin to start questioning her, too, so he waited.

The air was still quite cool at just after eight in the morning. The sun gently heated the fabric of his shirt, promising warmer temperatures ahead. It was the end of April, and they'd already seen the beginning of the spring storm season with a boisterous thunderstorm last week. John much preferred storm season to the unusual amount of snow they'd received over the winter.

Eve parked and got out of her car, a pair of dark sunglasses balanced perfectly on her nose shielding the expression in her eyes.

She walked toward him with purpose, the tight ponytail at the back of her head swinging with each step. The sun caught her red hair and accentuated the blonde highlights.

When she reached him, she tilted her head up to see his face. "Thanks for waiting."

"No problem." He led her toward the front of the building.

Even with her thick-soled sneakers, Eve was a good head shorter than he was. She wasn't necessarily what he would consider petite so much as compact. A word he was sure she'd hate, even though it was meant as a compliment. Of course, he'd never tell her that. Just like he wouldn't tell her how she looked in the jeans and dark green sweater she was wearing today, both articles of clothing gently accentuating her natural curves.

"Into the breach," he whispered, taking a deep breath of the crisp air before stepping inside. Thankfully, the room they were looking for was on the first floor.

She pressed her lips together and followed him inside to the apartment. She removed her sunglasses and slipped them into a pocket.

Caution tape marked off the open doorway ahead and to the left, but that didn't seem to deter the onlookers who tried to get as close as they could. Several officers stood on either side of the hallway to keep them from crowding the apartment entrance.

People naturally wanted to know what was going on. For some, it was simple curiosity. For others, they wanted to be the ones to pass along the news to their friends, whether the information they had was correct or not.

Most people, though, wanted to know whether they should be concerned for their own family and friends.

John certainly understood. Protecting the town was his priority, and that included those who meant the most to him. His passion was to solve cases and put the bad guys behind bars.

He felt for the officers who were handling the disgruntled group.

"Who's going to fix my bathtub now?"

"What about my water heater? I've got a newborn baby, and I need hot water that works!"

"The guy's lucky someone didn't kill him years ago."

One of the officers who stood at the doorway nodded at

John and Eve, lifted the tape so they could pass, then lowered it again.

The first thing John noted was that there was no sign of forced entry. A few feet past the door on the left, a small table had been knocked over, and the items that had been on top of it now littered the carpet. He took in the small living room that, the upended table aside, looked to be in a lot better shape than the rest of the building so far. It wasn't fancy, but it appeared clean, except for the lingering smell of cigarette smoke in the air. He wrinkled his nose.

He followed Eve to the other side of the room where Officer Jenny Durant was busy taking photographs of a man who had collapsed on the floor in front of his couch.

John steeled himself to take in the scene with a detective's eye and not just one of compassion and sorrow. It didn't matter how many years he'd been on the force—he never got used to seeing the victims.

He prayed he never would.

The man on the floor looked to be in his forties and sported a nasty cut on his left cheekbone. His thinning hair was disheveled, and his left arm was tucked under his torso in a way that looked unnatural. If he'd fallen on it, then he likely never regained consciousness afterward.

Jenny paused and turned toward them. "Hey, guys."

"Morning." Saying "good" in a situation like this was hardly appropriate. "Who do we have?"

"Meet Mack Yates, manager of the apartment complex. A tenant found the body almost an hour ago." She motioned across the way to where an older woman was speaking to Officer Clint Baker.

The poor witness looked shaken as she pointed in their direction.

"She was supposed to speak with Yates to discuss a

broken water heater, but he never showed up or answered his phone. When she reached his door, she realized it wasn't latched properly and went inside. Her scream drew several other residents, and the news spread like wildfire. We barely got here before the news van took up residence outside."

John's jaw tensed. He much preferred to have a little breathing room in an investigation before dealing with the press. Well, given the state of the outside of the building, he suspected most of the inside probably wasn't much better. If tenants had trouble getting the manager to fix things, someone had probably called the news hoping to shed some light on the problem. He couldn't blame them. He just wished they'd called a different station.

"I'm sure Crispin is champing at the bit for the possibility of a sob story to share. It'd be good for ratings."

"No doubt," Jenny said, her voice heavy with sarcasm.

They'd all had issues with Crispin in the past. The reporter was well known for making their jobs more difficult on a regular basis.

She tilted her head toward the victim. "If even half of what we're hearing from outside is true, then I doubt Yates here was very popular. Nothing obvious is missing. The television, DVD player, and computer are all still here."

"It certainly doesn't look like the scene of a robbery, or at least not a successful one." He watched as Eve approached the victim in full investigative mode. He stood nearby to watch but left her plenty of room to work.

Eve systematically examined the body, checking the man's wrists, hands, and fingernails. "No defensive wounds or obvious cause of death." Finally, she looked at John. "Do you mind helping me roll him to his side?"

John snagged a set of gloves from Jenny, then carefully

rolled Yates over. There was some light brown discoloration on the man's pale blue shirt. Eve lifted the shirt to reveal two burn marks on the man's back at kidney level. "Looks like someone used a Taser on him."

"It's certainly consistent with a Taser burn," Eve agreed. "An older model, since no AFID tags were left behind." When she'd finished examining Yates, she nodded again, and John helped her ease the body back into its original position. She motioned to the cut on his face. "This wound is fresh. We'll swab the area and hope some DNA evidence was left behind."

John pointed toward the front door. "It looks like Yates opened the door for his killer. At some point, the killer struck him, causing him to fall onto the table and knock it over."

"With no sign of defensive wounds, I'm guessing the killer used the Taser at that point. It's possible that the jolt from the Taser could have resulted in a heart attack, but I won't know for sure until I can get him into an autopsy room." She conducted several tests before standing back.

John knew she had become completely focused on her job, so it wasn't until she'd taken her gloves off that he spoke to her again. "Any guess on the time of death?"

"He couldn't have been killed more than four hours ago." She turned to Jenny. "Has transportation been arranged?"

"Yep, I called it in a few minutes ago."

"Thanks." Eve crossed her arms in front of her. "I'll go back to the precinct and wait for the body to arrive."

"Sounds good. Even if the actual death was unintentional, someone struck and then used a Taser on the man. From the sounds of the tenants outside, narrowing down the suspects may take some time." He stepped closer and lowered his voice so only she could hear him. "Are you sure you're okay after earlier?" He hated that he hadn't even had a chance to ask about the case from her past.

To her credit, she made direct eye contact and gave him a decisive nod. "I'll be fine. Thanks, John."

With that, she left the apartment.

Eve was strong and professional, but John suspected events had more of an effect on her than she wanted to admit. He made a mental note to check on her again once he got back to the precinct.

Chapter Two

There were enough disgruntled tenants that John tasked Officers Clint Baker and Philip Lopez to help him collect statements and conduct interviews. Meanwhile, with so many people milling about, he'd asked Jenny to take photos of the crowd as discretely as possible. There was a good chance that the person who killed Yates—whether accidentally or not—might feel safe enough to stick around and watch the investigation. Having photos could prove useful later.

John flipped his notebook to a new page and moved to the next tenant. As soon as the man saw John approach, he stood to his feet and stuck out a hand. "Victor Carson. I live up in 301." He pointed to the ceiling. "So, Yates is really dead, huh?"

The man didn't seem surprised.

"Yes, he is. I take it that's not a shock."

Mr. Carson grunted. "Not even the slightest. He's been letting this place fall apart around our ears. There are thirty-two apartments in this building, and I'm pretty sure someone living in every single one of them had an issue with Yates."

This had become a running theme with the people John had interviewed so far. He wrote notes as Mr. Carson elaborated, giving examples of how Yates managed to get away with not fixing a plumbing problem or increasing the rent. When tenants were asked if they'd spoken to the owner of the apartments, none of them even knew who it was.

Mr. Carson ran a hand through his hair. "Yates irritated me to no end, but I could put up with it because this place is in my budget, and it keeps a roof over my head. I live alone. But if I had a family to take care of and no hot water or a toilet that wasn't working, I'd have been livid. I don't condone killing the guy—don't get me wrong. I'm just saying, I don't envy you having to narrow down the suspects."

John wasn't looking forward to that, either. He asked the same question he'd asked every other person he had interviewed so far. "Did you see anyone unusual in the building? Someone who isn't normally here?"

Just because Mr. Yates was dead, and there were a lot of people angry at him, didn't mean John was content to assume it was a tenant who had used a Taser on the man.

Mr. Carson shook his head immediately. "I was upstairs in my place until I heard sirens. I wouldn't have seen anyone."

John jotted down a few last notes. "Thank you for your time, Mr. Carson."

"You're welcome." The man stood. "What about the apartments? What's going to happen with them?"

"I wish I had an answer for you. We've got people trying to track down the owner. I'm sure a new manager will be hired as soon as possible. One of our officers will be going through and listing every complaint, especially those that violate city codes."

Mr. Carson nodded, a look of relief on his face. "I appreciate that. Thank you, sir." He left the room.

John looked over his notes. So far, tenants had reported seeing someone from two package delivery services, one person delivering food, and a bouquet of flowers were brought in. And that was just from the people he'd spoken with. He wondered if Philip or Clint had had any better luck.

By the time they'd finished up the investigation, John was more than ready to get back to the station. He checked his phone when he arrived, but there was no notification from the lab concerning the package that Eve had received.

After leaving a few things in his office, he went to check on her.

John used the heavy metal door to enter the main room of the morgue. It normally remained unlocked during business hours so people could come and go as needed. But when Eve worked late, she often slid the deadbolt in place so she wouldn't have to worry about someone surprising her.

From there, other doors led to the refrigeration room, a family room, and a hallway. That hallway had doorways to two different autopsy rooms, an x-ray room, and eventually Eve's office at the end. Several of her technicians were milling around. Probably getting things ready for the next autopsy. John wondered where Mr. Yates was on the schedule.

John gave one of the techs a friendly wave and started down the hall. He spotted Eve sitting at her desk on the far side of the room. He knocked softly on the doorframe. Her attention shifted from her laptop screen to him.

She motioned for him to come inside.

John took in her office. She had a heavy walnut desk, a comfortable chair, plus a small table in one corner with two chairs. Even though it didn't have any windows, Eve had made a point of brightening the room with extra lighting, framed photo prints of sunrises and ocean scenes, and even a small desktop fountain. He imagined the bleakness of her profession was partly what drove her to create such a peaceful and cheerful workspace.

He took a seat in the chair opposite her desk.

Eve offered him a smile. "Hey. How'd it go after I left?"

"It's going to take a while to sort through everything." John filled her in a little on the investigation so far. "It'd help if there had been any cameras in the building. I suspect the lack of cameras was more about keeping Yates from getting caught doing something he wasn't supposed to than about the tenants' privacy." He studied her for a moment. "Can you tell me about the other case you mentioned this morning. The one that the flower reminded you of."

The moment the words were out of his mouth, Eve tensed and looked at something on the desk. Whatever happened, she didn't want to talk about it.

He felt bad about pushing for more information, but if someone was sending her packages that made her uncomfortable, he'd like to figure out who it was.

Eve's stomach clenched, and for a moment, she thought she might be sick. Apparently, her emotions were showing on her face because John reached across the desk to touch her arm.

"Are you okay?"

She focused on the warmth of his hand and tried to push her discomfort aside. She gave a single nod.

He obviously didn't believe her. "I don't appreciate it when someone harasses my friends."

She was familiar with that expression of his. It was a mixture of compassion and determination.

There was a reason why John was one of the best detectives on the force. Once he was assigned a case, he didn't stop until he closed it. And that included getting all the details from her. She dreaded the conversation, and there was a part of her that wanted to ignore the box and the stupid black rose and pretend she hadn't received them.

Her gut said differently. If she had to choose someone to look into this, it would be John.

Her mouth went dry while the palms of her hands grew moist. She wiped them off on the legs of her pants.

John tapped the top of the desk. "Wait here. I'm going to get you a bottle of water. Do you need anything else?"

"No, I'm good."

"I'll be right back."

Eve rested her head in her hands and took a deep breath. "God, you know how hard this is. Calm my spirit and mind. Please give us wisdom."

A few minutes later, John returned with two bottles of water and a paper plate laden with several doughnuts. She accepted the water, the cold bottle dripping with condensation.

Eve set it on the table, then moved it, a trail of moisture following like a snail trail.

"I know you said you didn't want anything else, but someone brought in three dozen doughnuts. Who am I to refuse?" He gave her a grin, then picked up one with maple frosting and took a large bite.

Eve was surprised to see one of her favorites in the mix. She loved the light texture of crullers, and they were rarely included when people bought doughnuts by the dozens. She really wasn't hungry but couldn't pass it up. She took a bite, and the sugary goodness melted on her tongue.

To John's credit, he didn't push her to talk about the case. Instead, they finished their doughnuts and laughed about the practical joke that some of the guys played on the chief for his birthday not long ago.

Having that extra time gave Eve the chance to gather her thoughts. And the sugar gave her a little surge of energy that she didn't realize she needed.

This wasn't a conversation she ever thought she'd have. Not after all these years. Some memories were best left packed away in a trunk and stored in the back of a dark closet. Except she didn't have that luxury anymore.

Eve sipped her water and took in a deep breath. "It wasn't a case I was technically involved in. Not from a professional standpoint, anyway." She paused. "The victim was my best friend and college roommate."

She could do this. She'd stick to the basics. Give the necessary details of the case. John could get the case files sent to him after that.

Help me get through this, God.

If she could keep it clinical, she could keep the whole thing locked away again where it belonged.

"I'm sorry to hear that, Eve." Compassion filled John's eyes. "Take your time."

Eve swallowed hard. "The murder took place eleven years ago in the Dallas area." She told him which college campus, and he jotted the information down. "Isabelle Perez and I were best friends out of high school. We decided on a college together and then made sure we were roommates in the dorm."

She took another sip of water, not because she was thirsty, but because she needed a minute. It'd been eleven years, but it still felt like yesterday.

"We were only a month into our sophomore year. I was supposed to meet her at our dorm before dinner and then walk over to the dining hall together. I got caught up in the lab and told her I'd meet her in the dining hall instead." Her voice broke. Oh, how she hated having to say all this out loud.

John looked like he wanted to say or do something, but he waited patiently for her to continue.

"Isabelle never made it." She would never forget the cacophony of sirens that had filled the air that night. Even though no one said anything, she'd had a terrible feeling that the sirens had something to do with Isabelle. Eve had rushed from the dining hall and back to their dorm where officers were setting up a perimeter. She broke through the line before they could stop her. "They found her body in our dorm."

"I can't even imagine what you went through, Eve. I'm so sorry." He reached across the table and gave her hand a gentle squeeze. "You reacted when you saw the flower in the box you received. Is that related somehow?"

"Whoever killed Isabelle had tossed a black rose on her body before leaving." She shivered. She'd seen her best friend lying on the floor of their room, an image she had never been able to erase from her mind. "Isabelle had been stabbed multiple times with what the police guessed was a small knife. But they never did find the murder weapon."

"Did they come up with any suspects?"

Eve blinked back the tears that blurred her vision. "They

interviewed everyone, from classmates and teachers to neighbors in our dorm. Nothing panned out. There was one guy who was interested in Isabelle. He even asked her out, but she wasn't interested. At the time, she wasn't interested in dating anyone. I noticed him multiple times after that. I'd catch him watching us, but the moment he realized it, he'd leave the area. I found it creepy, but it was all on campus. I mean, he was going there, too. It was hard to point a finger and say he was stalking her. But it happened enough that it made me uncomfortable."

"And you told the police about it."

She swiped at a stray tear before it could make its way down her cheek. "I did. Detective Zeller was great. We gave him a description of the guy. His name was Jackson Arends. The detective pulled him in for questions at least two times that I know of. But there was no evidence. The guy claimed he didn't have an interest in Isabelle. There was nothing tangible to link him to her murder." She sighed. "Without a murder weapon, motive, or a viable suspect, the case went cold."

As John wrote more in his notebook, the corners of his mouth pulled downward. "I'm sorry about your friend, Eve." He raised his gaze to her. "And to lose her like that without ever getting closure..."

Eve sniffed, willing her emotions into check. She shifted her weight in the chair and crossed one leg over the other. "I'm not sure how long you've been back in Destiny. Do you know the Perez family?"

"No, I don't think I do."

"Well, this tore the family apart. Isabelle had a younger sister, Anna, and an older brother, Miguel. Isabelle's parents never did get along very well anyway, and she shared stories that sounded like some neglectful behavior had been going on for years. Miguel left home five years or so before we graduated from high school. Just took off. I don't know that he ever came back, even to visit. After Isabelle died, her parents split up and left Destiny pretty much going in opposite directions."

Eve took a long drink of her water, then replaced the cap. "Poor Anna had just graduated high school. I don't know if neither parent invited her to go with them or if Anna just refused. But she ended up keeping the house and fending for herself after that."

"Wow, that's horribly sad. Does she still live here?"

Eve nodded. "She does. I know she bounced around from job to job for a while, but I think she works for one of the real estate companies now. We were never close, probably because she was always very quiet. But Isabelle was like a sister to me." The tears welled up again. She consciously pushed away the emotional thoughts building inside her.

John looked at his notes as he bounced the tip of the pen against the paper. "I'll put out a search for Jackson Arends. See what he's up to these days."

Eve pointed to her laptop. "That's what I was trying to do, but I'm afraid my sources aren't nearly as effective as yours are."

"Well, one way or another, I'll locate him. Was the detail about the rose in the newspaper?"

"Yes. Too many people in the dorm saw the rose as they were walking by the open doorway. Zeller couldn't have kept it quiet if he'd wanted to."

"What about you? Were you ever mentioned?"

She nodded. "I planned a candlelight vigil on campus for her. A local newspaper covered the event. Someone showed me the story after it came out, and it included a photo of me."

"Clearly, the article about your job is a sore point for our suspect. They could have started a background search on you. Once they located the articles surrounding Isabelle's death, and found your connection to her, they thought using a black rose would scare you."

"Well, they were wrong. It didn't scare me. Startled? Maybe. Made me angry? Absolutely." She took in a deep breath and released it slowly. "That article came out last month. Why are they targeting me? And why now?"

Chapter Three

"Eleven years is a long time," John acknowledged. If the person who killed Isabelle had wanted to hurt Eve too, then surely, they would have struck long before now. And if it was someone who was upset that Eve got her ten minutes of fame, then why wait a month before contacting her?

He glanced at the framed article hanging on the wall near her desk.

Eve followed his gaze. "Mom made that for me. Obviously, whoever sent the rose thinks the article is wrong and that I didn't deserve the attention that it brought me." She grunted. "Too bad they don't know how much I hated the whole thing. I don't like being in the spotlight. I was told it was good publicity and to go with it." She rolled her eyes. "It'll be the last time I ever do something like that."

"So they hated the article. But why? Do they have something against you personally? Or against what you do in a professional capacity?" John stood and went around her chair to read through it again. It was a wonderful tribute to Eve and her skills as a medical examiner. The case she'd helped solve had been one of his—and her assistance had been crucial.

The article was something she should be proud of.

"What if the suspect saw the article and got upset because you were essential in closing this case, but another one involving their loved one went unsolved? It could've been a case they knew you were the ME on. Once they started digging up information on you, they found the details about Isabelle and figured they'd bring that into the spotlight. Use it to shake you up."

"So we're looking at a copycat." Eve didn't seem convinced. She ran her hands over her hair, smoothing the red strands and then tightening her ponytail. "If this is truly about a case that has remained unsolved, and the suspect is upset about that, then why not ask me to take a second look at it? Or even force me to?"

John pulled up the photos of the box and note that he'd taken earlier. He zoomed in on the writing and placed the phone on the desk in front of them. He stood next to her chair, one hand propped against the edge of her desk.

"Nice article. But soon, they'll see the truth. The great Genevieve Marks will fall just like the rest of them."

"The rest of who?" Eve sounded frustrated. "Other medical examiners? People working with the police? Or victims? The meaning behind it changes the whole tone of the note." She waved at the phone. "I'd like to think it's just some bored teen with way too much time on his or her hands."

John felt the same way, but his gut said it was more than that. He wished he knew how much more.

Both of their phones pinged. Since John's was on, a notification popped up letting them know that the lab results from the box Eve had received had been sent to them both by e-mail.

John pocketed his phone and leaned forward, resting his arm across the top of Eve's chair. He was close enough to catch a whiff of the subtle fruity fragrance of her shampoo. He looked over her shoulder as Eve opened the e-mail on her laptop.

She read the result out loud. "No recoverable fingerprints were obtained from the envelope, paper, rose, or inside of the box. Postage stamps were all adhesive. The postmark was from here in Destiny." She leaned back into her chair. "Well, that's that. Whoever sent it could have easily dropped it off at the post office without talking to a soul."

"And clearly wore gloves while packing everything up," John agreed. He was disappointed with the results as well, though it didn't surprise him. "Maybe this was a one-time thing. You know, the person thought it might end up in the news or something."

"We can hope." She pinched the bridge of her nose and then rubbed her temple. "I'll be starting Mr. Yates's autopsy in the next hour. I'll let you know what I find out about the cause of death."

"I appreciate it. I've got a stack of witness statements to sift through. I'll see if I can find anything consistent among them." He also had every intention of running a search for Jackson Arends. It'd be good to know where the man had spent his time in the last month.

Once he was back in his office, John put in a call to the Dallas Police Department which had originally handled Isabelle's case. After letting the operator know what he was calling about, he waited nearly ten minutes before someone finally came back on the line.

"Good afternoon. This is Officer Ables. How can I help you?"

John explained again that he wanted to speak with the detective in charge of the Isabelle Perez case.

"I'm afraid that Detective Calvin Zeller is no longer with our department."

John squashed his disappointment. "Is there any way I can get copies of the case files?"

"Absolutely. I'll make sure they're sent to you as soon as possible." He paused. "I'm going to warn you, though. There's not a lot to go on. No real evidence. No murder weapon. No suspects. The case went cold fast, and Zeller never even got leads to follow up on. It was isolated. Random."

"Even still, any information you can share will be great. We've had an incident here that may be connected. On their own, there's not much. But together, maybe some common thread will present itself."

"I hope you're right, detective. These cold cases— they've never sat well with me. The victims deserve justice."

"I agree. I don't suppose you know where Detective Zeller is now, do you? In case a question arises that I need to speak to him directly about."

"I don't, but I'll ask around. Someone here may know where he went when he left."

Well, that was better than nothing. John nodded even though Ables couldn't see him. "I appreciate that. Thank you."

"You're welcome. Good luck."

The call ended, and John set the phone back on his desk. The screen darkened, catching the light from the ceiling above and reflecting it back at him.

He'd wait for the case files to come in, go through those,

and then see if there were any cases that Eve had a hand in that weren't resolved. Maybe one of them would stand out.

Meanwhile, he needed to weed through the dozens of people from the apartment building who had a motive to see if any of them had the means to kill Yates. It might not have looked like anything was taken from the victim's apartment, but the truth was, they might never know. There had to have been a reason for why someone used a Taser on the man.

Paul, one of Eve's technicians, wheeled a gurney from refrigeration through the main room and into one of their two autopsy rooms. He had been working with her for nearly two years, and his help was invaluable. There were many things she relied on him for, and that included assisting in the autopsy, weighing and cataloging organs, and just providing a second opinion.

Eve turned her attention to the decedent whose body was covered by a white sheet. "All right, Mr. Yates, we're going to get started here. If you have anything to tell us, we're more than ready to listen."

Thankfully, Paul was used to Eve's insistence on speaking to the decedents as though they were there listening. She believed that they deserved the utmost respect. She tried to treat them as though they were a living patient, being sure to explain what was coming up next in order to help them feel more comfortable. She liked to hope that whoever examined her best friend had offered her the same level of dignity.

Eve started her portable recording device and began with a detailed description of the appearance of the clothing as they removed everything for processing, including noting that there were some brown stains on his shirt where the Taser was pressed against it. Paul took photos of everything so they would have them later in case an article of clothing was called into evidence. A clean, soft blanket was placed on the decedent to preserve his dignity.

Eve put the same effort into listing any distinguishing marks or injuries on his body. She made sure to mention the burn marks from the Taser as well as a long, thick scar on his right leg. When she'd finished, they wheeled him into the radiography room.

Thanks to a huge donation a couple of years ago, they had a whole-body radiography station, making it possible to X-ray the entire body in a short amount of time. It was especially useful for gunshot victims, but Eve had found it essential for all trauma cases when it was difficult to tell what kind of damage was done.

Once the X-ray was taken, Eve combed through the images in case there was anything she needed to be aware of.

"Check this out." She called Paul over to the screen she was looking at. She pointed out the eight screws that held a metal plate in place along Yates's tibia from the base of the bone halfway up the shin.

Paul grimaced. "That must have been a nasty fracture."

Eve nodded. Based on the rate of healing and scar tissue, she guessed the break to have happened at least ten years ago. Maybe even longer. She refocused the X-ray on Mr. Yates's chest. "What else do you see here?"

To his credit, Paul took the time to really look over the X-ray before drawing a circle around the heart with one finger. "It's enlarged. Noticeably so."

"Very good. It likely indicates a preexisting condition

prior to experiencing an electrical shock from the Taser. We'll know more once we get in there and can examine the heart." They took blood and urine samples, and Eve had Paul run them to the lab so they could get started. Other tissue samples would be gathered throughout the autopsy as needed, and those would take much longer for results.

With nothing else to note, they began the autopsy. As usual, once Eve got into the process, the time seemed to disappear. She had more than one thing to share with John by the time they finished. Paul took the decedent back to the refrigeration room, cleaned most of the autopsy room, and then excused himself for lunch and a doctor's appointment.

Eve removed her gloves and dialed John's number on her cell phone.

"Hey." His voice sounded even deeper over the phone than it did in person. "How's it going?"

"We finished the autopsy. I thought you might like a report."

"Please. You'll be saving me from a sea of paperwork that's threatening to drown me. Besides, I have some things to share with you, too. I'll be right down."

Eve had just finished drying a bone saw and was putting it away when John's voice echoed in the room. "I'm sorry that took so long."

She jumped, one hand flying to her chest just below her neck. "You should announce yourself before coming in," she told him, her voice firmer than she'd intended. "It's dangerous down here." She motioned to the collection of knives and other tools resting on a nearby table, waiting to be stored in drawers once they were dry.

He looked contrite, but there was a hint of humor in his eyes as he took in the tools. "I'll remember that next time."

The sparkle was fleeting, though, and concern took its place. "You look tired."

"Gee, thanks." She wanted to tease him about looking tired, too, but that was far from the truth. With a thin layer of scruff on his face and that glimmer in his eyes, he appeared entirely too handsome for his own good. "Let's go to my office. My chair is calling my name."

John waited for Eve to sit behind her desk, then claimed the chair on the other side. He motioned for her to begin. "It sounds like the autopsy might have given us something to work with. What did you find?"

They'd worked many cases together, and she knew John wasn't squeamish. In fact, he generally preferred to see photos or illustrations to go along with any information she had to share.

While she opened her laptop and located the pictures that she wanted to show him, she said, "The lab has samples to run tests on. In addition to the usual toxicology panel, I'm having them run some other tests as well." She showed him a photo of the heart. "Mr. Yates was suffering from an enlarged heart, which often causes few to no symptoms, although we did note some mild edema, or extra fluid, in his legs. He had cardiomyopathy, which causes the muscle of the heart to become rigid or thick. The combination would make it harder for the heart to pump blood effectively."

"Even if he knew about it, I don't think any of his tenants did."

"It's possible he was never aware of it. A toxicology panel will let me know if he was taking any medication to help with it. Did you find any at his apartment?"

John shook his head. "Nothing prescribed."

"I want to wait until we get those blood test results back, but I'm feeling fairly confident in saying that the shock from the Taser was enough to throw his heart out of rhythm resulting in cardiac arrest and sudden death."

John rubbed his chin with the side of one of his fingers. "There was no sign of forced entry. Either Yates left the door unlocked, or he opened it himself. At some point, the suspect used the Taser. Maybe Yates went into cardiac arrest, which scared the suspect, who left before getting what they wanted."

"It sounds like a reasonable hypothesis. Did Mr. Yates have anyone in his life who could go through the apartment and note if anything had been stolen?"

"No wife, kids, or close family. I don't think we'll have any way of knowing if something was taken."

"That's just sad." Eve frowned.

She might not have any siblings, but she was close to her parents. She couldn't imagine going through life without family to lean on. She shook herself from her melancholy mood and went on with her report. "Aside from his enlarged heart, the only other thing to note was a severely broken leg some years ago." She told him about the plate, screws, and the thick scar that ran along the man's leg. "But I don't see how it'll have any relevance to this case unless it hindered his ability to get away from his attacker." She closed her laptop and set it aside. "Did anything stick out when you went through the tenant statements?"

"There were so many inconsistencies, you'd think most of these people lived in different towns instead of different apartments in the same building." He pulled out his note-book. "But there were three things that stood out. Several people claimed they saw a repairman come in an hour or so before Mr. Yates's body was found. Apparently, getting anything fixed in that apartment is like pulling teeth. After calling around, it turns out someone from the phone company was sent to repair the modem in the main office. He's been working for the company for over twenty years with nothing but high praise for a job well done. After speaking with him, I removed him from the suspect list."

Eve's stomach growled. She opened a drawer in her desk and took out a small package of cookies. She held them out to him, and he took two with a nod of thanks. After he'd eaten one of them, he continued.

"I had multiple reports of a nurse coming into the building. That turned out to be the daughter of one of the tenants on the third floor. She was bringing her mother's prescriptions by before going to work." He polished off the other cookie. "This last one has the most potential. I had five different people say they saw a delivery man come in with a package. I'm not sure which company he worked for, as those details varied, as did their description of him, but everyone said the package was about the size of a shoebox. Three people saw him enter the building, and two people saw him leave again. No idea where he went in between. The odd thing is, if the reports are accurate, he didn't leave the box but took it back out with him."

"That *is* strange. Maybe he wasn't allowed to leave it in the hallway if the resident wasn't home?"

"That's possible. I'm trying to find out if any of the local companies had a delivery to an address in that apartment building, but it's taking time to get that information." He leaned back in his chair and stretched his arms over his head before bringing them back down. "If someone had knocked on Mr. Yates's door claiming to have a package for him, I can see him opening it without hesitation."

Eve thought back on the number of times she'd looked through the door's peephole at home, recognized someone's uniform, and opened the door to accept a package without thinking twice. Between that and the creepy box she'd received earlier, she had to suppress the shudder that ran up the length of her spine.

She caught John watching her with an expression on his face that she couldn't quite interpret. "What is it?"

"I've started digging into Isabelle's case." He paused, probably waiting to see if she had any objections.

Truthfully, she wasn't sure how to feel. She was thankful that he was taking the black rose and note seriously. Yet the fact that he thought he should made her feel even more apprehensive about the meaning behind them.

"Okay." She nodded for him to continue.

A hint of relief flashed across his face before he went back into detective mode. "I've requested that copies of her case be sent here. I'm still waiting for those to come in. I am trying to get ahold of Detective Zeller, who is no longer working for the Dallas Police Department." He leaned forward, his expression growing serious. "I also did a search for Jackson Arends."

"Why do I get the feeling that I'm not going to like what you're about to tell me?" Her stomach clenched as she waited for him to elaborate.

"He was arrested on an unrelated charge about a year after Isabelle's death. He was convicted and sentenced to fifteen years in jail. He was released early on parole six months ago."

"I don't suppose we know where he is now?"

"He ditched his parole officer shortly after. His location is unknown, but he did once mention to his parole officer that he hated Texas and wanted to go back east to find his brother."

Eve's eyes slid shut as images of the way he'd watched them back on campus came to mind. The idea that the guy could be out there somewhere, focused on her, made her feel sick. She tried to take comfort in the possibility that he really had gone back east and was far, far away from Destiny.

The sensation of John's hand covering one of hers encouraged her to take a deep breath and open her eyes again to find him watching her, fierce determination etched into his features.

"We don't know yet that he's behind the box you received. It could be a crazy coincidence." His large hand gently squeezed hers, practically engulfing her much smaller one. "No matter who's behind this, I promise I won't let them touch you."

Chapter Four

He'd seen Eve in a variety of situations at work and during the infrequent casual gatherings that the precinct hosted. But never had John seen her look as vulnerable as she did now. He'd hated having to deliver the news that Jackson Arends was not only unaccounted for, but that the time he'd spent in jail could explain why there'd been such a long stretch between Isabelle's murder and the box that Eve received in the mail.

There was still a big part of him that hoped the box was an isolated event. But the fact that someone took the time to research the black rose and include that with the message told John they were looking for someone who intended to do harm, even if it was emotional and psychological rather than physical. The lack of fingerprints meant enough foresight to wear gloves.

Whatever the motive, he didn't want this person getting anywhere near Eve.

He meant what he said about keeping her safe.

His gaze caught on the cookie wrapper, then flicked to

the clock. It was after one. She had to be starving. Reluctantly, he let go of her hand. "Have you eaten lunch yet?"

She blinked at him, clearly surprised at the change in topic. "No. I haven't."

"Me, either. We can't fight crime on an empty stomach. I'm going to run and get us some sandwiches."

"That sounds amazing. I just have a few more things to clean up here. Let me get you some money." She opened a file drawer and started to take out her bag.

"Nope, lunch is on me. Meet me in conference room two in twenty minutes?"

"Thank you. I'll be there." She gave him a smile, and he was happy to see some of the stress and worry on her face ease.

Because it was after the lunch rush, it didn't take long to pick up their food. When John got back to the precinct and entered the conference room, he found Eve already there waiting for him, her laptop open in front of her. She motioned to the row of windows along one wall. "Every time I come in here, I'm tempted to take it over as my office." She chuckled then, and John's heart lurched.

The windows and the view had nothing on Eve's smile.

"You and me both. I figured we could both use a change of scenery while we ate." He was certainly tired of looking at the four walls of his own office. He held up a bag from his favorite sandwich shop in town. "Turkey, bacon, and ranch, right?" When her eyes widened in surprise, he simply shrugged and admitted, "I've noticed you've ordered it a few times in the past."

"Thank you for remembering." She reached out and accepted the sandwich. "I don't know whether to be flattered or if this is a sign that I need to branch out in my lunch choices."

"I see nothing wrong with your choices." He caught her gaze for a moment before she turned her focus to her food.

The moment Eve started eating her sandwich, her mood seemed to improve. He found that his did as well. He wondered if she'd eaten anything today besides the cookies and the donut earlier. At least John had claimed several slices of banana bread that Arnold brought in that morning. Pastries were a frequent treat lately because his wife, Chloe, was craving them during her pregnancy.

"Have you voted in the baby poll yet?" John asked.

The chief and Chloe were expecting their first baby in August. The next doctor's appointment was tomorrow, and the couple hoped to find out if they were having a boy or a girl. Someone in the department, though John hadn't heard who it was, had set up a box with ballots so people could write down their guess. Tomorrow morning, the results would be counted and then revealed, hopefully followed by the chief's announcement of the ultrasound results.

A note had gone out last week that people were welcome to bring food to contribute to a celebratory dessert bar. John had no doubt there would be enough sweets to feed everyone in the precinct if birthday celebrations there were any indication.

Eve wiped her mouth and grinned. "Yes, I did the first day the box was set up. Although I've never been very good at that sort of thing. Jenny and I are already planning the baby shower."

After the serious nature of the last day and a half, John enjoyed seeing Eve look so excited. "Is Jenny the one who set up the poll?"

She raised an eyebrow. "I am not at liberty to say."

But the slight upturn of her lips told him that it *was* Jenny, and that Eve might have even had a part in it as well.

"Well, I think it's very kind of you ladies to put such an effort into doing all of this for Chloe."

Eve smiled and shrugged as though it weren't a big deal.

Except it wasn't the first time he'd seen her go the extra mile for a co-worker. When Tia in dispatch was laid up for three weeks after surgery, it was Eve who had set up a meal train to ensure Tia didn't have to cook for the entire duration of her recovery.

It was Eve's outward beauty that had first snagged John's attention, but he quickly discovered she had an even more attractive personality. "So are you guessing boy or girl?"

"Girl." Eve didn't hesitate. "I just have a feeling. I pictured her with a girl the moment they announced the pregnancy. How about you?" She took another bite and watched him curiously.

"I guessed boy. Not for any real reason, though. I just wrote down the first one that came to mind."

They ate in silence for a while. These sandwiches were some of John's favorites. It was a bonus that the restaurant donated a small amount from every sale to the local fire department.

Eve took another bite of her sandwich and set it down. "I hope you're able to get in contact with Detective Zeller."

"Me, too. From what you said, I don't expect to get much information from the case files. But talking to the detective could give us some insight that was never made official." He took a drink of his Dr Pepper.

"I remember Isabelle's parents complaining that he wasn't doing a very good job with the investigation. But then again, they were very..." Eve seemed to consider her words. "They argued over everything. I'm not sure any investigation would have been up to their standards."

"It's too bad they don't still live here. Same with the brother, Miguel. It'd be worth talking to them." He reached for his sandwich and took another bite.

"I have no idea where Mr. and Mrs. Perez are, or Miguel. I doubt Anna does, either." She picked at her napkin, a frown appearing on her face. "I always felt so bad for her. I reached out afterward, but none of the family seemed to welcome my contact." She shrugged. "Sometimes I think they blame me for what happened."

There was something about the tone of her voice that had John instantly on alert. Did she blame herself as well? "Nothing about this is your fault, Eve. I'm sure they didn't think so, either. They were grieving. Maybe they didn't want to be reminded of what happened, so they pushed everyone and everything away. Sadly, it's a common reaction." He'd seen it many times.

There was a reason why families who lost a loved one to a violent crime were encouraged to seek counseling. It was a terrible thing to go through only made worse by added feelings of guilt.

He wondered if anyone recommended that Eve get counseling back in the day. He had a feeling that she might have been overlooked as Isabelle's best friend because she wasn't family.

She didn't seem convinced by his words, and he was trying to decide whether he should push or not when her eyes widened, and she literally dropped what was left of her sandwich.

"What is it?"

"Anna. I mean, let's assume Jackson is behind all of this. If he's put in the effort to scare me, what if Anna is on his radar, too?" She pushed her chair away from the table. "It's possible, right? John, we need to make sure she's okay."

Eve studied John as he turned west on Ninth Street. He'd tried to get her to stay at the precinct while he went to check on Anna, but Eve had insisted on going along. She had to. After all, Anna might be more inclined to share information with another woman present. She wasn't so sure he agreed, but he didn't tell her no.

"You can be very persuasive, Miss Marks. If you ever need a change in career, you should consider interrogation."

Eve laughed out loud at that. "Thanks, but no thanks."

"If anything seems amiss, I need you to stay in the car until I come back for you. Agreed?" When she didn't respond immediately, he gave her a sharp look. "I need you to stay safe, Eve." He took them down another side street.

"And I feel safer with you than I do anyone else." The words tumbled out as she thought them, and Eve immediately wished she hadn't spoken at all. Good grief, it made her sound like some helpless woman. Or even worse, a smitten teen. She fought back a groan.

According to the GPS in John's car, Anna's house was just up ahead on the right. It wasn't far, yet every second seemed to stretch along with the silence in the car. John pulled up in front of the older home and put his car in park.

"Hey." He tapped her arm with the back of his hand. When she turned her head, she found him watching her, his expression serious. "Your trust means a lot. I don't take it lightly." With that, he got out of the car and came around to open her door for her.

Eve had always known she could count on him both professionally and as a friend. But for the first time, she wondered what it would be like to be that special someone in his life. To have his love and devotion. One thing was certain, that woman would be blessed.

Their hands lingered together a second or two longer than necessary, and Eve truthfully didn't know if it was because she was reluctant to move hers or if it was on his end.

John kept his head on a swivel, looking up and down the street before studying the small house in front of them. All the while, he stayed right next to her, his hand lightly touching her lower back. "Nothing seems off," he murmured.

They climbed the rickety stairs that led to a narrow porch, and John rang the doorbell.

All at once, memories of seeing Isabelle on the floor in their dorm room flooded Eve's mind. She tried to shut them out. Maybe she should have waited in the car. *Please, God, help Anna to be okay.*

As soon as the door opened, and Anna Perez took a step through the doorway, Eve's system flooded with relief.

Anna looked surprised to see her and a little confused. "Eve?" Her gaze shifted over Eve's shoulder to John. "What are you guys doing here?"

John introduced himself. "Do you mind if we come inside for a few minutes?"

When Anna didn't look convinced, Eve reached out and put a hand on the other woman's arm. "Please?"

Anna finally gave a nod and took a step back, ushering them inside before closing the door again. She led them to the living room and waited for them to take a seat on the small couch. "What is this about?" She sat in an old chair nearby.

For the first time, Eve wondered how Anna and her family found out about Isabelle. Did they get a call from campus security or the police? Or did someone come to the door to personally inform them of their loss?

Eve could imagine how painful it must have been. While they hadn't been friends in high school, she had still attended many school events with both Isabelle and Anna.

John leaned forward. "Have you received any odd or threatening phone calls, notes, or messages lately?"

Anna's eyebrows drew together. "No." She reached for her cell phone and checked the main screen. "Why? Who would be sending something like that?" The words were spoken slowly, as though she were afraid of the answer. "You two are making me nervous."

When Eve glanced at John, he nodded, letting her know that she should take point. "We ask because I received an odd package in the mail this morning, and there is a reference to what happened to Isabelle." She didn't want to give any specifics. "We still don't know if it's truly connected to Isabelle's case or if someone is pulling a malicious prank. But we wanted to make sure no one was harassing you."

Anna clasped her hands in her lap. "No. Nothing at all. Who would do something so horrible?" She shook her head. "I wouldn't even know how to reach my parents at this point to see if someone was bothering them about Isabelle. I don't know that they'd care."

"So you don't think they'd try to contact you and warn you?" The question came from John.

"Maybe. I truly don't know. I haven't spoken to them regularly in years." There was no missing the sadness in her voice. "My mom was in the hospital with pneumonia two years ago. I found out about it nine months after the fact, if that tells you anything."

Eve couldn't imagine walking away from a child and not looking back, especially not after what happened to Isabelle.

Everything about Anna's family situation was gut-wrenching. Eve kicked herself for not trying to reach out to Anna more. Even if the efforts weren't welcome, she could at least try.

"What about Miguel? Are you guys in touch?"

Anna shook her head. "No. I think he lives in Corpus Christi." She shrugged. "I used to have his number, but it's changed since then."

"Well, we're glad that you're okay." John gave her an encouraging smile.

"Yeah, I'm fine." Anna fiddled with the hem of her shirt.

John looked to Eve, sensing they were wearing out their welcome.

"Thank you so much for speaking with us," John told her as he stood. "I'm glad you haven't had any trouble. I'll track down your family if I can and make sure they're not getting any threats either."

He pulled a card out of his wallet with his contact information. "If you do have any questions or concerns, please don't hesitate to call me or reach out to Eve. Hopefully, it all turns out to be a non-issue."

Anna took the card and lightly tapped it against her knee. "Thank you." She looked from John to Eve. "You be safe, okay?" There was a barely perceptible catch in her voice.

Eve suspected there was more that Anna wanted to say, but she remained quiet as she walked them to the door.

"I'm sorry we just barged in here. Thanks for listening. You be safe, too. And seriously, call either of us if you need anything." Eve held out a hand for John's card and wrote her own phone number on the back before handing it to Anna again.

"I will."

They said their goodbyes. Eve had just buckled herself in when John slid into the driver's seat.

"I can't imagine being all alone like that," Eve said, her voice low. "I mean, when I left home and moved to Destiny, it was so weird being here without my parents. And it's only an hour and a half away. To not even know where your parents live..."

"I can't imagine, either." John took a last look at Anna's house and started the car. "It's just me and my parents. I don't have siblings. But we're close. Whether by blood or choice, family is everything."

Eve nodded thoughtfully. As they pulled away from Anna's house, she couldn't help but worry about her. "Just because she hasn't received a threatening letter yet doesn't mean she won't."

"I was thinking the same thing."

Except there was little they could do when they didn't even know for sure who was behind it.

Eve's phone rang, and Paul's name popped up on the screen. She answered it and immediately put it on speaker. "Hey, Paul. I'm here with Detective Paris."

"Perfect. The toxicology report came back. Are you guys headed in?"

"We're on our way now," John told him.

"Great, I'll have it waiting for you at the morgue when you get here."

Chapter Five

John wondered what information the toxicology report would have. With any luck at all, it'd give him another avenue to investigate.

They rode in comfortable silence on their way back to the station. He glanced at Eve, who seemed to be deep in her own thoughts. The woman was independent. And stubborn. Two traits he found particularly attractive. More than that, though, she handled everything today with grace and determination. Not that it surprised him, but it did reinforce the respect he already had for her.

Once they arrived at the station, they immediately headed to the morgue. Paul met them at the door, a laptop tucked under one arm.

"Welcome back." He set the computer up on a counter. "First, the lab finished going over Mr. Yates's clothing. The brown stains were caused by a Taser, but I think we all knew that. There were no surprises and nothing else that would be considered evidence in the case. Unfortunately, there was no secondary DNA in Yates's wound, either."

That was disappointing. John had hoped the killer

might've left behind hair or fibers or some other form of DNA that might be used to identify them.

"Let me pull the toxicology report up for you guys." Once he did, he started reading through the results, pointing at each line as he did so. "No drugs or alcohol in Mr. Yates's system. Upon your request, Dr. Marks, they tested for various medications that the deceased might have taken to manage his heart condition. None were detected."

Eve leaned against the counter and pointed to another set of results farther down. "Troponin levels were raised, suggesting a myocardial infarction did, indeed, occur after Mr. Yates was tased."

Paul nodded. "There's one more odd set of results." He scrolled down through the document, then stopped and pointed.

Eve's brows rose in surprise, but John had no idea what they were looking at. "What is it?"

"In a healthy human, the body produces C-peptides and insulin at a one-to-one ratio. Mr. Yates's insulin levels are practically off-the-charts high. Alone, that would be odd. But his C-peptides are low."

John looked from the results to Eve. "What does that mean?"

Eve pushed away from the counter and turned. "It means that he received insulin from some external source. His levels were so high that it likely led to hypoglycemia. Since his heart wasn't in great condition to start with, he then had a heart attack. I think there's a higher possibility that the hypoglycemia was a direct cause of the heart attack over the Taser." She shook her head, clearly deep in thought. "But you said you didn't see any medications in his apartment. And we didn't find any indication that he gave himself insulin shots." She frowned. "Paul, please bring Mr. Yates's body to autopsy room one."

"Yes, ma'am."

Eve motioned for John to follow her into the next room.

"What are you thinking?" he asked her.

"That I missed something during the autopsy." She bit down on her lower lip as they waited for Paul to come back with the decedent.

When Paul pushed the gurney into the room, John stepped back to give them space to work.

"Paul, would you hand me a magnifying glass, please?"

The technician did as she asked while she donned a pair of gloves.

Eve lifted the white sheet to reveal Mr. Yates's feet, moved a light to shine on them, and leaned in closer. "I checked his feet during the autopsy, but since there was no evidence of drug abuse, I didn't expect to find any marks between his toes," she explained. But a moment later, she shook her head and leaned away from the body. "Injecting that amount of insulin would normally leave a decent bruise..."

The expression on her face changed from one of confusion to satisfaction. She pulled the sheet back further to reveal Mr. Yate's right leg. She held the magnifying glass over the thick scar that ran along the length of his lower leg. "There. Right there." She handed the magnifying glass to Paul. "What do you see?"

Paul's brows lifted as he looked through the magnifying glass. "Injection marks. I count six of them."

"Yes." Eve nodded as she practically bounced on her heels with excitement. She took the magnifying glass from Paul and handed it to John so he could look, too.

It took a moment to spot the injection sites, but once he

knew what he was looking for, he also counted six. "Wow, no wonder you missed those."

"I would never expect someone to inject anything like that in the leg. The extensive scar tissue likely reduced any bruising that might have occurred. Couple that with the possibility Mr. Yates suffered a heart attack shortly after, quickly reducing blood flow to the area, and it's no wonder we couldn't see them."

"Which means someone used a Taser to incapacitate Mr. Yates, and then proceeded to inject insulin into his body, which ultimately led to his death." John couldn't believe it. "He was murdered."

"Without a doubt." Eve turned to Paul. "I need you to get pictures of these injection sites, please. And then excise part of that tissue. The lab should be able to test for the presence of insulin where it was injected into the skin."

"How hard is it to get your hands on that much insulin?"

"Unless it's been prescribed, very difficult."

John latched onto a theory. "Is it possible to have insulin mailed to you? Or do you have to pick it up from a pharmacy?"

"There are plenty of online pharmacies that could send insulin to patients by mail."

That's what John hoped she was going to say. He put an arm around her shoulders and gave her a quick hug. "You're amazing! I need to get to my office."

Her brows creased in confusion. "What are you going to do?"

"I'm going to call around and see if anyone reported a missing shipment of insulin," he hollered back as he jogged down the hall.

The television in the break room was turned on and tuned into one of the local news stations. Eve watched as John stepped in front of a crowd of reporters and began to speak into the microphone.

"We have been able to confirm that Mack Yates, manager of the Gale Apartments, was murdered. While no one has been arrested yet, we do have a person of interest. We're looking for a white male in his late twenties or early thirties. We believe he may have been posing as a delivery person to get into the building. He might have stolen that package either off a truck or from a porch. If you saw anyone matching this description in the area of the apartment building this morning, or have any other information, please give us a call."

John went on to give out the phone number for the tip line.

"We are considering this an active case and will continue to pursue all avenues until the person responsible for Mr. Yates's death is in custody. That's all I have for now. Thank you."

John gave the crowd of reporters a nod before stepping away from the microphone.

"I don't know how he does it," Jenny said.

"Me, either." Eve had come in for a cup of coffee and found Jenny taking a break, so she decided to join her. Eve admired John's ability to get up there in front of people and still look cool as a cucumber. "I thought I was going to pass out with nerves when they interviewed me for that article." Seriously, she was jittery for days beforehand.

Jenny lifted her cup and then downed the rest of her

coffee. "I also can't believe someone managed to intercept a box of prescription insulin. How does that even happen?"

"One of the drivers failed to lock her truck when she went to find someone to sign for the medication deliveries at the hospital. Apparently, it was taken right out of the back, although we can't say for sure it's the missing insulin we're looking for. I'm pretty sure the delivery driver won't make that mistake again, and I'm guessing the whole company is going to crack down on securing packages before delivery."

There'd been more insulin in that package than the killer had used on Mr. Yates. Knowing he still had some was not a comforting thought.

"I'm excited to find out if the chief and Chloe are having a boy or girl tomorrow." Jenny clapped her hands together. "We'll have to get together in another month or so and plan out the baby shower."

Eve was more than happy to switch gears to a happier topic. "Most definitely. Once we know the gender, we can start picking up decorations and things like that." Except if Eve was right, and they were having a girl, she'd insist on more than just pink in the color scheme. Purple, green, and blue were all great colors, too. There was just something about babies and the new beginnings they represented. She couldn't wait to hold her.

That was one thing about being an only child. If Eve had siblings, she might have been an aunt by now. As it was, she rarely got to hold a baby unless it was for someone at church.

Eve covered a yawn. "Oh, I shouldn't have sat down. That was a mistake."

Jenny chuckled. "Tired?"

"Exhausted." She glanced at the clock. She could head home in an hour, and she was looking forward to it.

"I really wish all of this wasn't necessary." Eve crossed her arms in front of her and stood in the doorway of her home. John was just outside, the toes of his shoes touching the threshold.

"Me, too. But I'd feel better if you let me do a quick check of your house. Make sure no one messed with it." They'd already stopped by her mailbox. Thankfully, no strange packages were waiting for her.

Eve stepped aside. "Come on in."

He raised an eyebrow at her but didn't hesitate to walk right past her. She waited at the door while he went from room to room, verifying that the windows were locked and no one else was in the house.

"Are you sure you're okay here by yourself?" John didn't look convinced. "I'm sure someone from the station could stay here with you. Maybe Jenny? You don't have to stay here alone."

"I'm fine. You went through and checked everything out. I promise I won't be opening doors for strange delivery people anytime soon."

John looked like he wanted to argue with her. Instead, he pointed at her. "If anything worries you—no matter how small—I want you to call me. I don't care what time of night it is. Agreed?"

She wanted to counter his statement, but if the roles were reversed, she would feel the same way. "Agreed."

"Okay." He hesitated. "Try to get some rest tonight."

"I will. You do the same."

John waited on the porch until she'd closed the door and locked it. She looked out the window to see him walking back to his vehicle. He cast one last look in her direction, noticed her at the window, and gave her a wave. Even though the wave itself was friendly, there was a concerned look on his face.

She returned the gesture, then let the curtains close.

Now that she was in the house alone, it felt way too quiet. The ticking of the wall clock nearly echoed in the room until the heater kicked on, the sudden sound causing Eve to jump.

"This is ridiculous," she muttered to herself.

If this were a normal night, she'd get herself a quick dinner, grab a shower, and then fall asleep while a comforting TV show she'd seen a million times played in the background.

Dinner was easy enough. She threw together a sandwich and munched on it while she checked her e-mails. But she decided to forego the shower. All the movies and TV shows where a killer snuck into a house while the victim was in the shower came to mind. No, she wasn't scared. She wasn't worried someone was going to try and get into her house. But she was woman enough to admit she was jumpy. The last thing she needed was to be startled in the shower and fall. Then she'd have to call 9-1-1, only to have them rescue her while she was naked and cold on the bathroom tile. No, thank you.

The randomness of her own thoughts gave her a chuckle.

Instead, she settled for washing her hair in the kitchen sink. By the time she'd finished that, the day had caught up with her.

With a towel wrapped around her wet hair, she brought up *Friends*, crawled under the sheet and thick blanket on her bed, and settled in for an episode or two. With any luck, she'd be asleep within the hour.

And after the day she'd had, she sure could use some sleep.

Sometime later, Eve awoke with a start, confused. It took a moment to realize her phone was ringing, and it was the sound in combination with the vibration near her hip, that had startled her so much. She had to untangle it from the blanket and then, afraid she was going to miss the call, answered it without looking at the caller ID. "This is Eve."

She fully expected it to be her parents, John, or someone else from the police station. When no one responded, she pulled the phone away from her ear and saw "unknown" on the screen. Her pulse jumped.

This time, she put the phone to her ear and said "hello" one more time. Again, no one answered, but she could hear something moving in the background.

Creeped out, she punched End Call and tossed the phone onto her bed. A quick glance around the room assured her that everything was in its place. An episode was still playing, and based on the time on the phone, she'd been asleep for nearly an hour.

It was probably a wrong number. It wasn't like she didn't get those. Though, admittedly, they usually didn't say "unknown." As much as she'd like to go back to sleep, that wasn't happening right away.

Instead, she got out of bed, pulled on a sweatshirt and some socks, and combed out her hair. After that, she padded her way to the kitchen. What she needed was a cup of peppermint tea.

Eve had barely put the water on to boil when her phone rang again. This time, it was in one of the pockets of her pajama pants. Again, "unknown" stared back at her.

She took in a steadying breath, answered, and simply said, "Hello?"

No one responded, but a moment later, the sound of a ticking clock came through the receiver. Eve hung up, as angry as she was unsettled.

It could be anyone or anything. A kid playing a prank. Some weird issue with the phone line.

Who was she trying to fool? Someone was attempting to freak her out. Why else would they be calling her at nearly midnight? And the clock ticking? Creepy.

Eve focused on making her cup of tea. In the following ten minutes, two more calls came in. When the caller ID said the same as before, Eve rejected them immediately. She took her tea, got back in bed, and turned up the TV.

It was impossible to ignore the frequent calls coming in, though. Nearly every ten minutes.

She'd simply silence her phone, except she needed to be available in the event John needed her for the case, or her parents needed to get in contact with her. After an hour went by, the sound of her phone ringing had her going crazy. Clearly, whoever this was had no life or need to sleep.

As much as she didn't want to bother John, she couldn't allow this to go on forever. She didn't think they could trace an unknown number, but she had to give it a try.

Cringing, she dialed John's number.

He picked up on the first ring. "Eve?" She expected him to sound sleepy, but he seemed as alert as ever. "Is everything okay?"

"I'm sorry to bother you. But someone keeps prank calling me tonight. Is it possible to trace a number that's coming up as unknown?"

There was some rustling in the background. "What's the person saying? Can you hear anything?"

"Just the ticking of a clock." She paused. "I'm not going to lie. It's weirding me out."

"No joke. Okay, I'm heading your way. When we hang up, I don't want you answering any calls coming in from that same number. I'll call the station on the way and ask them to trace any incoming calls to your phone." There was the slamming of a door from John's end of the phone. "After I get there, you'll answer the next call and then keep it open for as long as possible. We'll see if the number the person is calling from can be traced." The rumble of the car's engine signaled he was on his way. "Are you good?"

"Yeah. Yeah, I'm good."

"I'll be there in ten minutes. Hang tight."

With that, he hung up the phone. Even with the TV on, suddenly everything seemed quiet. Way too quiet. Eve was seriously second-guessing her decision not to accept John's offer of having Jenny come and stay with her.

She tried to focus on the TV. It was the *Friends* episode, "The One with All the Cheesecakes." It was difficult to relax, but watching Chandler and Rachel eat cheesecake off the floor was enough to give her a chuckle.

Her phone pinged, the sound causing her to jump. It was a text, and when she swiped to read it, the hair on the back of her neck stood on end.

> "You and that detective figured out the insulin. Let's see if you can give a repeat performance."

The text was followed by a photo of a black flower.

Chapter Six

The drive to Eve's house seemed to take an eternity. John had entertained the possibility of just sitting outside her place in his car all night to make sure no one bothered her. Instead, he had told himself she would be upset if she found out. But once he got home, it'd been nearly impossible to settle down enough to fall asleep.

As soon as her call came through, he had kicked himself for not following his instinct and staying anyway.

He hit two red lights on the way over. After making sure the roads were clear, he drove right through both. When he pulled up in front of her house, he was relieved to see that everything looked okay. The porch light was on, as were the lights inside.

He sent Eve a text. "I'm right outside."

Seconds later, he could see the curtain move to the side as Eve peeked out to make sure it was him.

"Good job, Eve." It made him feel better to see she was being so cautious.

She opened the door wide enough for him to get inside,

then closed and locked it again. The ringing of her cell phone punctuated the air. Eve's arms were crossed in front of her, and she absently rubbed them with her palms. Even in the warm room with a thick, light blue sweatshirt on, she looked like she was freezing.

"What happened?"

Her gaze shifted to the offending device sitting on the coffee table nearby. She picked it up, her hands shaking, then handed it to him. "I got this right after I called you." Her voice sounded tight. Stressed.

John accepted the phone and zeroed in on the text. He ground his teeth together as he read the message. Afraid he might crush the phone out of anger, he tossed it onto the couch. "He knew about the insulin injections. We didn't release that detail to the press."

"Then the person who killed Mr. Yates..."

"...is the same person who mailed that box to you."

"I'm sensing a package theme here," Eve said, her voice laced with sarcasm.

"The vague description of the man who may have killed Mr. Yates could also fit Jackson Arends."

"And a fourth of the other men in town. This could still be a copycat situation. Maybe someone didn't like the way I looked at them when I passed them on the street." Eve was exaggerating, but the meaning behind what she said wasn't wrong. "We don't know for sure that Jackson is behind any of this." She shivered.

John placed a hand on each of her shoulders. "I promise you that we're going to figure this out."

"If this is all some sick game, does that mean he killed Mr. Yates just to get to me? What if he kills someone else?" Her voice caught.

"Eve." He waited for her to raise her chin and look at him. "*We* are going to figure this out."

This time, when she nodded, the tension in her face eased a little.

"I can go check around the outside of the house..."

"No. There's no way he's still there, if he ever was. Please, just stay in for now."

"Okay." He slipped an arm around her shoulders. With the other hand, he got out his phone and dialed the station. He spoke with dispatch to have a patrol go by the house every hour for the rest of the night.

John hung up and slipped the phone back into his pocket. He might have put his arms around Eve and pulled her in for a proper hug if her phone hadn't started ringing again.

Eve clapped her hands over her ears. "I don't know how much more of this I can take. I'd turn it off, except my parents wouldn't be able to reach me."

He knew what she meant. He always had his phone on as well. "Come on, let's sit down."

She lowered herself onto the couch and then he sat next to her. She stared at the ringing phone, the vibration causing it to move ever so slightly on the surface of the couch.

"Logan is at the station, ready to trace the next call you answer. When you do, put the phone on speaker and say hello. Then leave the call open until the other person hangs up."

The phone fell silent. He noted that the screen said she'd missed eight calls. No wonder she was on edge. Now that it wasn't ringing, the room seemed eerily quiet.

He looked to Eve and found her with a hand on each knee as though bracing herself. Her hair, which normally pulled into a ponytail, hung loose around her shoulders, the ends still slightly damp. He'd always thought her beautiful, but seeing her like this, casual and at home... He didn't often get the chance to spend time with her when they weren't on the job. It made him want to reach over and feel her hair between his fingers.

He imagined taking her out to dinner or going to see a movie. Doing something together, just the two of them. He wondered if that was something she might be open to.

Maybe, once the case was closed, he'd see what she thought about the idea.

Right now, he needed to get her through this. He covered one of her hands with his own, surprised by how cold her skin was. "You've got this."

She gave him a nod that didn't appear all that convincing. He squeezed her hand, hoping to remind her that she wasn't dealing with this alone.

Less than five minutes later, her phone came to life again. Eve jumped a little before reaching over to answer it and then switched it to speaker. "Hello?"

No response, but just like Eve reported, the sound of a ticking clock began. If he wasn't mistaken, the caller was holding the phone up to a recording of a clock rather than a physical clock in the room. The ticking was way too rhythmic and clear. He listened closely, hoping to detect some other noise in the background that might give them a clue to the caller's location.

Unfortunately, no other sound came through. It went on for just over thirty seconds before the call ended. "Good job," he told her as he took the phone. "Let's see if Logan found anything."

Eve nodded, then rubbed her hands together. He couldn't tell if it was because she was nervous or cold, but he spotted a colorful blanket draped over the chair on the other side of the room. He dialed Logan's number, then retrieved the blanket while his phone rang. As soon as he shook it out over her lap, she clutched it closer, burying her hands in the soft fabric.

Logan Alcott was one of the most talented technical experts that John had ever worked with. When he answered the phone, John put the call on speaker. "Give us some good news, Logan."

"The call came from a burner phone, so between that and the duration of the call, I couldn't trace it. However, I'm going to see if I can figure out which phone was used and where it was purchased. Most people use cash when they buy a burner phone, but maybe we'll luck out, and there'll be some kind of record. I'll get back to you tomorrow on that." He paused, and some shuffling sounded in the background. "I did pull up the logs for your phone, Eve. You've received a total of 23 calls this evening. All from the same number."

Eve wrinkled her nose at the news. It wasn't what John was hoping for either, but at least it was better than nothing. Maybe they'd be able to turn up more details tomorrow. "I appreciate it, Logan."

"Not a problem. Let me know if you need anything else."

The call ended.

Eve's phone began to ring again. John scooped it up and handed it to her. "Here, put it on silent. There is no need to listen to that all night."

"What if someone from the station needs to contact me? Or my parents?"

"I'll call dispatch and have your calls temporarily forward to my phone number. Why don't you send your parents a text, let them know you're having some trouble with your phone, and give them my number in case they need to get ahold of you." He called and left specific instructions for dispatch. Then he called and left a message for Arnold, telling him what was going on and that he'd be in that morning to give an official update.

He was relieved to see Eve had followed his advice. She placed the phone on its charger on the island, screen down, so she couldn't see the calls coming in. "Surely this maniac has to sleep, too," she said, her voice sounding weary.

"One would think." He wished he could do something to ease her exhaustion. "Why don't you go try and get some rest?" At this point, he had no intention of leaving Eve alone. If she insisted, then he'd spend the rest of the night out in his car in front of her house.

"I don't think I can. At least not yet." She studied him for a moment. "You're staying." It wasn't a question, just a statement.

"Yep. I just need to grab something from my car."

He thought for sure she'd tell him it wasn't necessary. Instead, she tipped her head toward the small TV in the living room where they sat. "In that case, I hope you like *Friends* reruns."

"Sure. I can pivot with the best of them."

That earned him a laugh and a tired smile. "Good man."

By the time he'd retrieved a packed duffel bag, she'd queued up an episode and was waiting for him with a blanket and two kinds of chips.

They didn't even make it through a second episode before Eve fell asleep.

John retrieved a pillow from her bedroom and gently lifted her head so he could place it beneath. "There we go," he said in a whisper.

Eve's eyes fluttered open just long enough for her to

focus on him before they closed again. She snuggled into the pillow. John said a silent prayer that she'd get some good rest. He made sure the blanket covered her still form, then found another for himself. He'd sleep in the recliner where he could make sure she was safe and that nothing bothered her for the rest of the night.

Eve was slow to wake. Even before opening her eyes, everything seemed different. Until the events of the night before came trickling back in. The last thing she remembered was watching TV in the living room with John. He must have turned it off because the room was silent now. She opened her eyes to see she was still on the couch, except she had a pillow under her head and the blanket pulled up to her shoulders.

She raised her head to find John lounging in the recliner, the footrest up. Seeing him there—and knowing he'd been present all night—calmed her instantly. She'd been half afraid to fall asleep last night, worried bad dreams would plague her. But she didn't think she'd moved a muscle—all thanks to the handsome detective who insisted on staying.

His eyes opened slowly, and he immediately focused on her. Eve felt her cheeks warm as soon as she realized he'd caught her staring at him.

He lowered the footrest and sat up with a groan. "Did you sleep okay?"

"I did." She sat up herself and stretched. "I'm sorry you got stuck sleeping in the recliner."

"If you had any idea how many times I've been on a long stakeout in my car, you'd know the recliner was a vast improvement." John stood up. He retrieved her phone from the bar and studied the screen before handing it to her. "Looks like over twenty missed calls. But the last one was just after three, so at least the caller gave up after a while. No more texts."

Eve took the phone and unlocked it. She scrolled through the missed calls to make sure none had been from her parents or the station. "Seriously, did he think I was going to just answer every single one and listen to a clock tick? He had to have realized I was going to silence it eventually."

"He's playing games. Trying to get into your head."

Well, if that was the goal, Eve was starting to worry that it was working.

She didn't even notice John had joined her until he nudged her elbow with his, drawing her gaze to his face. "Hey. Someone who's this desperate is reacting emotionally, not logically. That means he's going to mess up eventually. Trust me, Eve, we're going to catch him."

"Yeah. I hope you're right."

"I am. Now, come on, are you usually this depressing first thing in the morning?"

Eve was tempted to smack him on the arm but reconsidered. She had dragon breath, her hair was likely a mess, and she was finding the morning version of John with all that stubble way too appealing.

"Before I get my coffee? Who isn't?" With a smile that she hoped looked casual, she turned away from him. "I'm going to go change and get cleaned up. You can use the second bathroom down the hall."

John reached for the duffel bag he'd brought in. "Thanks. How about we grab some breakfast and coffee before we go to work?"

"That sounds great." Eve ducked into her bedroom and shut the door. It was still early, and getting something to eat just made sense. So why was her heart racing a mile a minute thinking about going out for breakfast with John? She got ready in record time, emerging from her room as she tightened the ponytail at the back of her head.

John must have brought a shaving kit along with his clothes because he was waiting for her, clean-shaven, and ready to go. Had he thrown it all together after she called? Or did he always have a bag waiting just in case? Since he made the comment about stakeouts, she guessed the latter.

"I was thinking we could stop by the Corner Café. Does that sound good?"

"Sure. I'll follow you there." The brilliant smile he flashed her stayed with her on the drive over.

Once inside, they claimed a table in the corner. They hadn't been there but a minute when a man walked up. He wore a t-shirt sporting the café's logo. Tattoos ran up each of his arms and disappeared beneath the sleeves.

He extended a hand to John. "Good to see you. Been a while."

"Yeah, work's been crazy." John motioned to Eve. "This is Eve Marks. Eve, this is Dean Shaw, owner of this outstanding establishment."

She shook Dean's hand. "It's nice to meet you. This is one of my favorite restaurants in town."

Dean gave her a grateful nod. "I appreciate that. What can we get for you?"

John ordered biscuits and gravy with a side of bacon. Eve chose a stack of pancakes with sausage.

"You got it. And I'll have that coffee out in just a sec."

Eve was impressed that Dean didn't carry anything to

write their orders on. She leaned forward and lowered her voice. "How do you guys know each other?"

"He's always been supportive of the police department. Regularly brings food or coffee by when we're working particularly tough cases. He's had a rough past, but he's a good guy. Memory like a steel trap."

Dean returned with a pot of coffee and two mugs. He filled the cups, made sure they didn't need anything else, and left again.

Eve wrapped her hands around the mug and took a sip. "That's exactly what I needed," she said with a happy sigh. She realized John was watching her, and her cheeks warmed. "Now you know that good coffee is one of my weaknesses."

He laughed then, a hint of something she couldn't quite identify in his eyes. "I'll be sure to remember that."

They fell into comfortable conversation, and it wasn't long before Dean brought their food over.

Eve couldn't remember the last time she'd had pancakes. These were especially good. John's food must have been, too, because there was a lot more eating than talking for a while.

She was just finishing her sausage when her phone rang. A glance at the screen told her it was the station. "This is Eve."

"Hey, Eve. This is Jenny. I know you're probably on your way in, but I wanted to give you a heads up. Another box is here for you. It looks very similar to the one you got yesterday."

The food she had eaten suddenly felt like a boulder in her stomach. She set her fork down, leaving the rest of the sausage uneaten. John must have sensed the change in her mood because he'd already flagged Dean down and quickly handed him a thin stack of folded bills to pay for their meal.

"Thanks, Jenny. I'll be there in ten." She hung up and pushed her chair away from the table. "He sent me another box," she told John.

He gave a terse nod, placed a hand against her back, and guided her out of the café.

Chapter Seven

The new box was slightly smaller than a shoebox. It had been taped shut and covered with stamps. Eve's name and the precinct address were printed on the label exactly like the first one.

John watched as Eve put on gloves and then took out her pocketknife to carefully cut the tape. This time, instead of being in the break room, they were in a conference room with the chief, Jenny, Clint, and Officer Gabe Harrison in attendance as well as Gabe's K-9 partner, Loki.

As soon as John had reported about the calls and text Eve received, Arnold set up a meeting. But first, they needed to know if the contents of the box changed anything.

Eve folded the knife and slipped it back into her pocket. "Here we go," she muttered.

Once the lid had been lifted and set aside, all they could see was white tissue paper. She took it out and handed it to Clint, who was bagging it all to take to the lab for analysis.

If Eve was nervous, she hid it well.

The last piece of tissue paper was removed to reveal

four black roses bound together at the stems with what looked like a bread tie. Another fancy envelope was tucked beneath them, making it necessary for Eve to move the stems aside to get to it. She held it in one hand and slid the box and its contents toward Clint.

He went through to make sure there was nothing left. Satisfied, he carefully laid the tissue paper on top of the roses.

Eve opened the envelope and pulled a piece of paper out. She cleared her throat and began to read the note.

"You found the first. Two more to go. Don't worry, I won't forget about you. You will be the grand finale."

By the time she'd finished, there was a slight waver in her voice. She held the paper and envelope out to Clint as though she couldn't get rid of them fast enough.

Jenny stepped forward and gave Eve a hug. "We are not going to let him get to you," she said fiercely.

"No, we are not." Arnold gave Clint a nod. "Take that down to the lab. Grab Logan. Meeting begins in ten minutes." He reached over and gave Eve's arm a gentle squeeze on his way out.

Eve said something to Jenny and then left the conference room.

John moved to stand next to Jenny. "Is she okay?"

"She said she was going to her office for a few minutes."

He hesitated. This was one of those instances where he wasn't sure whether he should follow her or give her some space.

Jenny must have sensed his uncertainty. She tilted her head toward the door. "Go."

"Thanks." He jogged to the morgue. When he entered the main room, no one was there. He was about to go to Eve's office when he noticed the door to the refrigeration room was open. He found Eve just inside the doorway, her arms crossed tightly in front of her. He was about to announce his presence when she spoke, her voice just above a whisper.

"I'm sorry, Mr. Yates." She paused, and her shoulders drooped. "If he wasn't after me, then maybe you would still be alive."

"Don't." John strode into the room, his voice echoing off the walls. "His death is not your responsibility."

"I know that. Realistically, I do. But the killer is after me, John. Me. Yates was likely a random pawn in this messed-up game. In the end, if it weren't for me, he wouldn't be lying here right now." Eve balled up her fists. "I wish this guy would just focus on me and leave everyone else alone."

"Whoever this is, he's obviously not sane. It's possible he might have killed Yates—or someone else—whether he had drawn you into the middle of it or not." John waved a hand toward the body. "You can't blame yourself for this."

Eve looked like she wanted to argue with him.

He held up a hand to stop her and continued. "It's okay to mourn. It's okay to be angry—you have every right to be. I know I am. I'm angry that this monster thinks it's okay to end someone's life and terrorize our town like this. I'm furious that he is targeting you and making you doubt yourself." He took several large steps toward her until they were practically toe to toe. "But don't you dare try to take any credit for what this person has done. It's on him. *Him*. Because the moment you place even a sliver of the blame on yourself, you allow him to have a level of control over you."

Her chin gave a barely perceptible quiver as she lifted it, her jaw clenching in response to his words. She opened her mouth to say something but pressed her lips together instead. She nodded once, then turned away from him.

John shifted so he was standing behind her and put his hand on her shoulder. She leaned into his touch, her upper back resting against his chest. The instinct to wrap an arm around her waist and pull her close was so strong that it shocked him.

Another moment and he might have, but Eve cleared her throat, swiped at her cheek, and moved away from him. Did she feel this connection between them, too?

Right now, they both needed something tangible to focus on. "The chief is waiting for us."

Eve nodded and sniffed. "Yeah. I just needed a minute to pull myself together."

"You can take as long as you need. I'll go back and let them know you'll join us as soon as you can."

"It's okay. I should be there, too."

When they got back to the conference room, everyone else was waiting for them, including Dr. Gerard, a psychologist whom they consulted with regularly.

The chief held up his hand to quiet everyone. "I think we can all agree that we're quickly approaching serial killer status. If this individual is, in fact, responsible for Isabelle Perez's murder eleven years ago, then one could argue that we're already there. The last thing I want is for this guy to tack on any more bodies to his resume. The mayor is going to be less than thrilled when he gets this update." The look on his face expressed what John, and probably everyone else, was thinking.

Once the public got wind of a potential serial killer, it was going to lead to panic. Not to mention, this guy seemed to enjoy the attention. The less they could give him, the better.

Arnold motioned toward Clint. "Why don't you start us off. Update us on the packages that Eve has received so far."

Clint reported on the box yesterday as well as the one she'd just opened. "It's down at the lab now. But given the lack of evidence with the first box, I'll be surprised if there's anything we can use."

Arnold turned to Logan. "Have you had any luck tracing the calls?"

"The caller used a standard burner phone. I was able to trace the purchase to a gas station in the Dallas area. The owner of the station said it was sold for cash and that there is no video footage available from that time."

The chief focused on Eve. "We know a package of insulin was stolen, and presumably, some of that was used on Mr. Yates. How much of that do you think is left?"

"If the same amount is used on another victim that he used on Mr. Yates, then we're looking at one more murder attempt. Maybe two. The thing is, there are so many variables in play. Each person has a different insulin level to start with. I'm not convinced that Mr. Yates would have died from the dosage he received if he hadn't had heart trouble in the first place."

John updated everyone on his investigation into Mr. Yates's death and the tenants at the apartment building. "Yates didn't have many friends, but I have been unable to find a solid suspect from the apartment building. His tenants were more likely to go in and punch the guy. A Taser and insulin? I can't see it." He flipped through files. "I should be receiving the files from Isabelle Perez's case sometime today, and I'm trying to get in touch with the detective who led the investigation. I'm hoping that something will help us connect that case with Yates. Right now, all we know for sure is that the person who killed Yates is focused on Eve and that he at least knows about the Perez case."

When everyone remained silent, Arnold motioned for Dr. Gerard to weigh in on the conversation.

The psychologist spoke up from where he was sitting. "Reading the case files for the Perez murder will be helpful. However, I did go through and read all the news reports as well as what Ms. Marks has stated about the case." He gave Eve a sympathetic nod. "I believe the person who killed Isabelle was angry. The murder was premeditated but not necessarily fully planned. The individual, most likely a man, grabbed a knife and went in search of the victim, and then killed her at the first opportunity to do so." He ran a hand over his bald head thoughtfully. "If one of the suspects at the time, Jackson Arends, is the person responsible, then his stint in jail may have led him to hyperfocus on the crime he did get away with, and that circled around to an obsession with Ms. Marks."

Arnold leaned back in his seat. "If it is Arends, then why has the MO changed? We'll need the case files to be certain, but from my understanding, there were no stalker-like incidences toward Isabelle prior to the murder. No deliveries. No messages." He looked to Eve. "Is that correct?"

To Eve's credit, she didn't flinch at the question.

"That's right. Isabelle and I lived in the same dorm room. We never had trouble with anything remotely related to stalking. No one bothered either of us, left notes, or anything else of that nature. The only reason why Jackson Arends stood out was because we both noticed him on several occasions after he asked Isabelle out, and she turned him down. Each time, he kept staring at Isabelle. But if we made eye contact with him, he'd take off." Eve lifted both hands, palms up. "Other than considering the guy odd, I didn't think much about it. Until afterward."

Dr. Gerard looked thoughtful. "It could be that Isabelle's murder was personal. He felt she'd slighted him somehow. Or maybe he had feelings for her that she didn't return. Whoever it was clearly sought Isabelle out with the purpose of killing her that night." He picked up a pen and silently twiddled it between his first and second fingers. "Again, assuming this is Jackson Arends, it's possible that spending time in jail made him feel powerless. When he saw that article about you, Ms. Marks, it only reinforced that. You moved on with your life. He did not. Leaving the black roses, sending you packages, and attempting to make you feel responsible for Mr. Yates's death are all classic tactics to assert some level of control."

That certainly seemed to track. John didn't like the idea of anyone seeking to control Eve. "So, was he hoping we'd figure out the true cause of Yates's death? Or did that mess with his plans?"

Dr. Gerard set the pen down on the table. "The problem with having control and feeling powerful is that you want others to recognize that, too. It's unclear whether the killer's goal is to rub in the fact that we don't officially know who he is or if he's hoping that he'll get caught so he can officially take credit." Dr. Gerard nodded as though he were agreeing with himself. "I think that, if you hadn't discovered the true cause of death, the killer would've pointed it out eventually."

The chief turned to Dr. Gerard. "What kind of personality are we looking at here? Can you give us any other insight into what we might be dealing with? Are we looking for someone who is criminally insane?"

The doctor pressed his palms together and rested his

chin on the tips of his fingers. "Most serial killers have some kind of personality disorder in play. To be considered criminally insane, the person committing murders would be doing so with no true understanding of the difference between right and wrong. The fact that this person is sending mail to Eve and making a game of it suggests a clear understanding of that difference." He seemed to think a moment before one eyebrow rose slightly. "I think we're looking at a sociopath who shows zero regard for the consequences of their actions. Clinically speaking, this person lacks remorse, demonstrates manipulative behavior, and shows impulsivity. In general, they don't have normal human empathy but are often incredibly good at pretending they do."

Eve's mind started running through everyone she or Isabelle knew at college to see if anyone matched that description. Even as first-year students, they had never been into the party scene. Most of their interactions with others were at meals or through classes.

At the time, it felt like Detective Zeller had interviewed them all at one point or another. He never seemed to find anyone that fit that bill. Or at least she assumed he hadn't.

"Would these behaviors have been obvious in children or young adults?"

"Not necessarily." Dr. Gerard held up a single finger. "While a psychopath is born with these behaviors due to underdeveloped impulse control and emotional centers of the brain," he held up a finger on the other hand and continued, "a sociopath is often developed over time in response to abuse, neglect, or trauma."

Then, it could be anyone. Eve was reminded of those murder mysteries where all the guests at a party realized that someone in the room with them must be the killer.

"Let's set aside the possibility that Jackson is behind this. How on earth are we supposed to find this person?" Eve didn't realize she'd spoken the question aloud until everyone was looking at her.

Dr. Gerard didn't seem to think twice about the question. "We're looking for someone who killed Mr. Yates and is trying to control you because it helps him feel something. This person will enjoy having power over others. This can manifest itself in three different ways, but I think we're looking at a power/control process-focused killer. Someone who feels important because they are manipulating someone else in one way or another. One of the best ways to bring out a person like this is to compliment or critique what they've done. They are often quick to either accept credit or defend their work."

His words sank into Eve like an anchor in the water, causing anger to swirl like the silt being disturbed below. She was the one being manipulated. This maniac was threatening to kill at least two more people and then take her out as some sort of grand finale. What if they didn't stop him in time? What if her parents got back from their anniversary cruise before they caught him, and he decided to turn his focus on her family?

John leaned forward. "How likely is the killer to follow through with his threats?"

"It goes back to this person needing to feel in control. I'd say highly likely."

Eve spoke up. "What if this is a copycat?"

Dr. Gerard tilted his head slightly to one side. "If someone tends to be oriented toward violence, then reading about Isabelle's death may have been an inspiration. Most people who are convicted of a copycat murder were already mentally unstable before they started killing. Reading or hearing about the original crime acts more like a rudder rather than a trigger. He probably already had the why, but it's the details from Isabelle's case that might be inspiring the answer to how."

It was a lot of information, and Eve struggled not to feel overwhelmed. They had more insight into what might be going on in the mind of the murderer, but how were they supposed to actually find him?

"Eve?"

She jumped when someone touched her arm, only to find John watching her with concern. "I'm sorry. What did I miss?"

Arnold was kind enough to pretend like she hadn't zoned out. "As frustrating as it is, we need to keep an officer with you at all times." He gave Eve an apologetic look. "We're not taking any chances. This guy is desperate and cocky. He's going to make a mistake, and we're going to be there when he does."

A chorus of "yes, sirs" echoed from around the table.

As much as Eve dreaded the thought of having someone stand guard around her, knowing she wouldn't be alone was also a comfort.

The chief gave a satisfied nod and stood. "But for now, I've got an excited wife waiting for me to pick her up and a doctor's appointment to get to." He smiled then, and the mood in the room lightened considerably. "We'll stop by before I take her back home and officially declare a winner in the gender vote."

"What about you, boss?" The question came from Clint. "What's your guess?"

"Whatever it is, I have a fifty-fifty chance of being right." Arnold chuckled. "I'll be back in an hour or so. Do me a favor and solve this case while I'm gone, huh?" He dismissed everyone and left with a wave and a definite bounce to his step.

His excitement eased Eve's anxiety. She'd always liked the chief, but once he and Chloe became a couple, they'd all seen a whole new side to him. The chief doted on his wife, and it was clear she thought the world of him, too. Their joy over welcoming a new member of the family in a few months was contagious.

There was still a remnant of a smile on Eve's face when someone came into the conference room with a large file box in his arms. "Hey, Detective Paris, this was just dropped off for you."

John accepted the box and turned to Eve. "These should be Isabelle's case files. If you're up to it, we could go to my office and look through them. See if anything stands out."

"Sure."

The sooner they could find a real connection between Isabelle's death and Yates's, the better.

Chapter Eight

It didn't take long looking at the case files to see that Detective Zeller had been thorough with his investigation. John read every detail, hoping something that seemed like nothing back then might have some significance now.

Of course, there was always the possibility that the man who killed Yates and was bothering Eve was only using the black rose because he figured it would get under her skin. The idea that this may be someone else entirely was something John had to consider.

He looked up from the paper he was reading and watched Eve for a moment. She was staring intently at her own stack of paperwork while absently scratching her head near where the band kept her ponytail in place.

John pictured how she'd looked last night and this morning with her hair down around her shoulders. He thought she looked beautiful all the time, but that had quickly become his favorite way she wore her hair.

He forced his focus back to the files in front of him. He

had a rolling whiteboard set up in his office, and when either of them had found a relevant detail, they'd written it down so they could keep track of it. He stood and started adding three names: Jackson Arends, Miguel Perez, and a janitor from the dorm by the name of Carl Trevor. He'd been looking at local small-time criminals as well who had recently been released from prison. Maybe someone who didn't like law enforcement in general, but no one stood out to him.

Eve read the names on the board and shifted her focus to him. "Did you find something?"

"These are the individuals that Detective Zeller questioned more than once." John tapped the last name with the cap of his dry-erase marker. "According to this, Carl had made several of the women in the dorm uncomfortable. They claimed he lingered near the bathrooms longer than necessary." He looked at Eve. "Do you recall seeing him? Or having any concerns about a janitor?"

"No." Eve set the file she was reading down on her lap. "I remember Detective Zeller asking me about him back then, too. If I met the guy, I sure don't remember. And if there was someone lingering around the restrooms or our dorm, I'm quite certain we would have noticed."

He was sure she was right. He tapped Miguel's name. "I wonder why they questioned Miguel twice when they didn't do the same with Anna or their parents. Especially if any form of neglect was a possibility."

"It doesn't mean Anna or Miguel would've said something about that, though. Chances are, the detective had no idea."

"True." John pressed the marker lid against his chin. "I'd sure like to ask Zeller why he pulled Miguel in for a second conversation." He hoped the officer he spoke with at the Dallas Police Department would be able to track the detective down.

"Why? What are you thinking?"

"I'm keeping in mind what Dr. Gerard said earlier. About how a sociopath is developed over time through childhood, and often in response to abuse or some kind of traumatic event. We know there's a possibility that Mr. and Mrs. Perez were at least neglectful parents."

Eve wrinkled her nose at the thought. "If things were that bad, I'd like to think Isabelle would've said something. We were best friends. Practically sisters. We told each other everything."

"Miguel is quite a bit older than Isabelle and Anna. You mentioned he left home years before you and Isabelle graduated high school."

"Then there's a possibility that any abuse he might have suffered happened before Isabelle was even aware of it." Eve sounded doubtful.

"Do you think you'd recognize Miguel if you ran into him on the street?"

"Honestly? I don't think I would."

Then, as far as John was concerned, Miguel was a person of interest. Certainly at least until he could provide a solid alibi for Yates's time of death. "I'll check into Carl Trevor's whereabouts. See what he's been up to for the last eleven years. And I had planned to track down Miguel and make sure he isn't receiving any threats. It'll give me a chance to get a feel for the guy."

With that said, they went back to looking at the files, but there was little more information that they didn't already know.

Eve finished going through her stack of files and set

them on the corner of his desk. Her eyes looked tired, and she released a soft sigh.

"Hey, I know it's nothing definitive. But we have more now than we did before. At least we have further proof that Zeller was suspicious of Jackson. Carl is worth looking into as well." So was Miguel, but John could tell that the idea Isabelle's own brother might have murdered her didn't sit well with Eve.

He lifted her stack of files, added them to his, and placed them all back in the box. "So what made you want to become a medical examiner? Is it something you always wanted to do?"

She laughed at that. "Most definitely not. I was going to go into nursing, actually. Same with Isabelle. But once she died, and her case continued to remain unsolved, I decided that I wanted to pursue a career that helped other families going through the same thing. Law enforcement wasn't for me, so becoming a medical examiner seemed like a natural direction to go in." She reached for a pen and balanced it across one finger. "I'm fortunate, though, that I'm able to work here and that I'm only one and a half hours away from my parents. There aren't a lot of locations in Texas with their own medical examiners."

It was even less common for morgues to be housed in the same building as the police department. Usually, they were located at the hospital.

The smile that was on her face a moment ago faded. "I'd be lying, though, if I said I hadn't wondered if I should have just stuck with nursing and stayed in my hometown. Especially the last couple of weeks."

"I'm glad you didn't," his response was immediate, and by the way her brows lifted, she was as surprised by his words as he was. "Think of all the cases you've helped solve. The families you've been able to give closure to."

She nodded slowly. "Although I'd like to hope that someone else would be here doing my job and providing the same service."

"I'm also certain we would have never met. And I, for one, am very glad we did." John realized his comment might have come off as flirting, but he meant every word of it. He didn't want to hide his interest and attraction anymore. The question was whether she felt the same way.

Her green eyes locked on his for a moment before her phone rang, keeping him from knowing the answer to his question.

She swiped the screen. "Hello?" The worry and stress on Eve's face evaporated nearly instantly. "Okay, we're on our way." She ended the call, a smile on her face. "That was Tia. The chief and Chloe just arrived. Everyone's gathering in conference room two."

Her excitement was palpable. After everything that had happened lately, she deserved something happy to focus on. They all did.

The conference room was packed when Arnold and Chloe entered. Eve remembered how, when the couple started dating over two years ago, Chloe had been incredibly shy. She still preferred to stay out of the spotlight, but the people at the precinct quickly won her over. Her excitement about the baby didn't hurt, either.

Arnold put an arm around his wife and drew her closer, eliciting several "Awwwwws" from around the room.

Tia held up a piece of paper, getting everyone's attention. "Several of us tallied the guesses. Sixty-five percent said the baby is a boy, and thirty-five percent said girl." She motioned toward Arnold to take over from there.

He looked down at Chloe, who nodded. He cleared his throat. "We're having a daughter." The couple grinned at each other, and Arnold leaned in to give his wife a kiss.

The room erupted in whoops and applause as people took turns shaking Arnold's hand.

Eve waited for her turn to give Chloe a hug. "Congratulations. I'm so incredibly happy for you."

"Thank you." Chloe beamed as she pressed a hand against her expanding waistline. "Everything looked great on the ultrasound. Now we just have to agree on a name."

"At least you still have some time." Eve lowered her voice. "But unless you want everyone to weigh in on the options, I'd definitely decide that between the two of you."

Chloe chuckled. "No doubt." She turned to her husband, who looked at her lovingly.

Eve felt a painful twist in her heart. She wasn't jealous of the couple, not even a little. She was thrilled for them. But what they had was something she wanted some day. Truthfully, it was something she thought she'd have had years ago.

She scanned the room as people visited and laughed, and her gaze stalled at John. He was standing across the room shaking Arnold's hand. As though he could sense her watching him, his attention shifted to focus on her. He gave her a little smile that threw her heart rate into overdrive.

Earlier, when he'd insisted that she not blame herself for Yates's death, and then he'd simply been there with her meant more than she could ever say.

It'd taken everything in her not to turn around and hug him.

The last two days had been rough. They would've been so much worse if John hadn't been standing by her side.

John's phone rang, and he answered it. He immediately looked at her as the relaxed expression on his face changed to show he'd gone back into detective mode. He stepped outside the conference room, and it took everything in Eve not to follow him. A minute or two later, he reappeared in the doorway and motioned for her to join him.

They rounded the corner into the hallway, where it wasn't as loud.

"That was Detective Zeller. I'm supposed to meet with him this afternoon, but he works in Houston now and is scheduled to appear in court for a case. I'll be driving down there to talk to him."

Eve's eyes widened. "That's, what, three hours each way?"

"Three and a half hours." John took a sip of his soda.

"Is there a reason he can't talk to you over the phone or even on a video call?"

"He says he has some personal notes that he'd like to hand over, and he doesn't feel comfortable doing so by text or e-mail. I agreed to meet him." He glanced at his watch. "I'm going to update the chief and then head that way."

Eve wanted to ask if she could go along. But if the killer struck again, then she'd be needed here. She prayed there wouldn't be another victim and that John would get information that would help the case.

"Did he give you any idea what was in the notes?"

"Not really. But the case went unsolved, and that's something that'll eat at a detective. Even if there's no actual evidence that was withheld from the official file, sometimes personal insight or even impressions are useful. I think it's worth the try."

She glanced at the shirt pocket where he kept his small notebook. "Do you do that? Keep notes about cases that never make it into the official files?"

"Yes, I do. Sometimes, my brain rushes over all kinds of possibilities, and it seems jumbled until I write it down. Most of the time, everything I write gets crossed out. But once in a while…"

"It leads to a break in the case."

John shrugged and studied her for a moment. "I'm not particularly fond of the idea of leaving you here. If anything happens, three and a half hours away sounds like an eternity."

"Then you'll just have to get there, talk to Zeller, and get back as fast as possible." She spoke softly, surprised by the mix of emotions swirling in her chest. She would be perfectly safe at the station, and John knew how to handle himself as well. But she really didn't like the idea of being so far apart.

He cleared his throat. "Will you do me a favor?"

"Of course."

"Be careful, stay safe, and don't ditch the people keeping an eye on you."

"No sneaking out the bathroom window. Got it." She made some kind of a sign with her hand meant to mimic what the Boy Scouts might do. She clearly got it wrong because John just chuckled. "I'll be fine."

"I know you will." He hesitated before turning and heading back into the conference room.

Their conversation earlier came to mind. Especially the part where John had told her he was glad she'd moved to Destiny because he wouldn't have met her otherwise.

Before she lost the courage, Eve called out, "Hey, John?" When he paused, she said, "For the record, I'm glad I moved here, too. Getting to know you is one of the highlights of living in Destiny."

He flashed a grin over his shoulder. "Good to know."

Chapter Nine

For better or worse, a long drive meant plenty of time to think. John had gone over the details of the case in his mind from start to finish. What bothered him the most was not seeing a clear motive for why Eve had been targeted. Obviously, the killer was upset with Eve for one reason or another. John couldn't imagine it would be something personal—at least nothing Eve could have done intentionally. Even if it was, were they looking at something from the past, or was it related to a recent case?

His thoughts shifted to what Eve said before he left the morgue... Did he dare hope that she might be open to going out with him when all of this was over?

John could hardly wait to get back to the station and see her again. What would it be like to have her to come home to every day? To wake up next to?

He longed to get married one day and have a family. His parents had certainly been asking him about it a lot lately. Given he was their only chance for grandkids, he really couldn't blame them. But he'd never found someone he could imagine himself spending the rest of his life with.

Until Eve. It was easy to picture a future together. Far too easy. It helped that he'd known her for several years. He'd always kept his interest casual, but for the first time, he regretted not saying anything before. Where would they be now if he had?

"God, I have no idea where this is going. I pray that you help me to find some answers for this case, and that you'll keep Eve safe in the meanwhile. Guide us through everything else when this is all over. Thank you, Father. Amen."

He was two hours outside of Destiny when his phone rang. He pressed the button on the car's console to answer via Bluetooth connection.

"This is Detective Paris."

"Um, yeah, this is Miguel Perez. You left a message saying you wanted to speak with me." The other man's deep voice filled the cab of the car. "You said it's about my sister Isabelle's case."

John had tracked down a number for Miguel and left a message yesterday. He'd started to wonder whether the man was going to call him back at all. He briefly explained that he was investigating a series of murders in Destiny in which Isabelle's case had been referenced. "At this point, we suspect a copycat situation. But since your sister's case was never solved, a direct connection is possible. Have you received any threatening notes or calls in the last week?"

"No. Nothing."

"What about any unusual activity around your home? Is there anything that you're concerned about?"

"Everything has been normal here." There was a moment of silence. "Have you checked on Anna?"

"I spoke to her already, and she's fine."

"I'm glad she's okay."

"Do you happen to know how I can get ahold of your parents?"

"I have no clue. I've only spoken to them a handful of times in the last eighteen years." There was no missing the bitterness in his voice. "I couldn't even tell you if they're both still living at this point."

"I understand there were a lot of relationship issues in your family when you moved away. Would it be possible for you to elaborate on any of that?"

"Growing up, my home was a nightmare. My dad couldn't hold a job and drank away what little money he did bring in. Then he'd take out his own failings on me. My mom clearly preferred Isabelle over Anna and me, though I never understood why. But as far as Mom was concerned, Isabelle could do no wrong. When I left, I offered to take Isabelle and Anna with me. Do what I could to get them away from the caustic environment. Isabelle refused. She was going off to college anyway. And Anna? She never stood up for herself. So I walked away, and I never looked back."

Miguel made it sound like a decision that had been easy for him, but John wasn't fooled. There was no way a guy could walk away from two younger sisters knowing they might be next in line for his dad's anger and never second guess that decision.

"Did your father ever physically harm you or either of your sisters?" The fact was, they had no idea where the father was and therefore couldn't eliminate him as a suspect, either. However, he *was* originally eliminated in the investigation into Isabelle's death.

"There was a lot of verbal abuse and neglect, but no, he never physically harmed us. If he had, I wouldn't have left my sisters behind."

"When was the last time you talked to either of your sisters?"

A moment of silence preceded Miguel's reply. "I spoke to Isabelle on the night she graduated from high school. I'm not sure about Anna. It's been a long time."

"I know this hasn't been easy, and I appreciate your time. I only have a few more questions for you. First, when was the last time you were in Destiny?"

"I haven't stepped a toenail in that town since the day I left."

"And where were you this last Monday morning?"

Miguel grunted. "I work for a construction company here in Corpus. I clocked in at the site at five that morning." He gave the name of the company. "You're welcome to verify that with them."

"I'll do that. Thank you again for your time. If you do receive any threats, please contact me."

"I will." Miguel paused. "Do I need to worry about Anna? Is she in any danger?"

"At this point, we don't believe so. We've set up a patrol to go down her street regularly until we've caught the person behind all of this." John took Miguel's concern for his sister as a good sign. He had a feeling the man's alibi would pan out, but he still had to check it out to make sure. "Thanks again. Have a good day, sir."

"Yep. You, too."

The call ended, and John tapped against the steering wheel with his thumbs. A moment later, he used voice command to dial Eve's number. The sound of her voice brought a smile to his face.

"Hey. You get to Houston already?"

John chuckled. "I wish." He filled her in on his conversation with Miguel. "It sounds like his family was less than nurturing, and maybe that fits somewhat with the kind of upbringing that Dr. Gerard said could contribute to the development of a sociopath. But I didn't pick up on that with him. I'll be curious to see what kind of an impression Zeller had, and why he interviewed Miguel twice."

"I'm curious, too. Anna reached out to me with a text a little while ago." Eve sounded surprised. "She was wondering if we could meet for lunch or something soon."

"How are you feeling about that?"

There was a pause. John could almost picture her green eyes looking off to the side as she considered the possibility.

"Honestly, I'm surprised. She didn't seem all that happy to see me when we checked on her. But I think Isabelle would have been happy to see us reconnect. I'll probably give it a chance. I can't know until I try, right?"

"Right."

Anna seemed incredibly lonely. Maybe if she and Eve spoke again, it would be healing for them both.

"Hey, John. Hold on a sec." There were muffled voices in the background and the sound of something shuffling until Eve spoke again. "There may be another victim. A woman was found by her employer. He thought she was dead, but when an ambulance arrived, there was still a pulse. They're taking her to the hospital now."

A knot formed in the pit of John's stomach. "What makes you think this is related?"

"She'd been tased. There's nothing missing in the house. Whoever did it got in and out without anyone seeing him. I just have a feeling." There was more scuffling in the background. "I need to get to the hospital. If she's been injected with insulin, then they need to know immediately."

Man, John wished he were there with her. He didn't like the idea of her investigating any of this when the guy who was after her was still out there. "Is Jenny there with you?"

"She hasn't let me out of her sight since you left." There was a hint of humor in Eve's voice. "We're getting ready to head out."

"I need you to promise me that you'll be careful, Eve. I'm serious."

"I know. I promise."

"Let me speak to Jenny real fast."

"Drive safe, John." Her voice was muffled for a second as she spoke to someone else. "Here she is."

After some shuffling and tapping sounds, Jenny's voice came over the line. "Durant here."

"Hey, Jenny. What's the plan?"

"We're going over to the hospital shortly. Clint heard the doctor mention the possibility of the patient being in a coma. If this is related to Yates, then Eve's impressions and thoughts could be hugely helpful."

John didn't doubt that. "Is the hospital room secure?"

"Clint has made sure of that."

"Let me know what you guys find out. I've still got a way to go until I enter Houston. I won't be back to Destiny until late tonight."

"We'll keep you updated." She said something to someone else on her end. "All right, we're ready to head out. Don't worry. We've got this."

"I know you do." And he did—he trusted Jenny and everyone else there to do their best to keep Eve safe.

It was the rampaging serial killer he didn't trust.

Eve squelched the nervousness that rose in her chest as they entered the hospital. She couldn't quite shrug off the feeling that someone was watching them. Ignoring the instinct to look around her as they walked, she tried to draw comfort in the fact that she had Jenny on one side and another officer by the name of Carrington on the other. It felt like too much, honestly, as though they were drawing too much attention.

Surely, whoever was after her wasn't just waiting around a hospital for her to walk by.

But then again, wasn't the unpredictability of it all part of the problem?

After taking the elevator up three stories and going down several hallways, Eve was relieved to see Officer Clint Baker ahead. He was sitting in a chair outside of a closed room. When he saw them, he got to his feet.

"We've got a Leah Garrity resting inside," Clint began as he took out his notes. "She works for a local house-cleaning business and has been there for over five years. Thirty-nine. Single mom to a twelve-year-old daughter who is staying with a neighbor until the family can fly in from Maine."

Eve immediately felt sorry for the poor girl. She had to be frightened, not knowing how her mom was doing. "What do we know about Leah?"

"She was cleaning a house for one of her regular customers. The owner, Owen Geoffries, got home after work and was surprised to see her car still parked outside. Normally, she took care of everything before he got home. When he went inside, he found her lying on the floor in the living room and called 9-1-1." Something caught Clint's attention. He looked down the hall and waved at a doctor who quickly changed trajectory to join them. "Geoffries originally thought that Leah was dead, but when an ambulance arrived, they found a pulse."

Clint introduced everyone and moved to stand outside the room. Dr. Gia took over describing what was going on with Leah.

"Miss Garrity came in unresponsive. En route to the hospital, it was discovered that she is diabetic and had been fitted with an insulin pump. The level of insulin in her bloodstream was high enough to put her into a hypoglycemic coma. Her respiratory rate and heart rate had fallen to the point that it was nearly undetectable."

If the owner of the house hadn't come home when he did, Leah likely wouldn't have made it. "Do you think she'll come out of the coma?"

The doctor thought a moment. "There's always a chance. I've seen it happen before. We're working to get her insulin levels stabilized right now."

Eve nodded and said a silent prayer of thanks that the poor woman had survived and prayed she would make it through the ordeal. "Can we go back inside and examine the patient?"

Dr. Gia's brows rose.

Eve motioned to the room behind them. "If we could go inside, I'll explain the situation to you."

"Of course."

Once in the room where there was more privacy, Eve told the doctor about Yates and the insulin injections that resulted in his death. "Much like Miss Garrity, Mr. Yates was also shocked with a Taser. What I'm looking for is evidence that the person who attacked her also injected her with insulin." She silently studied the woman who had many wires and tubes running from her body to various machines. Her skin was pale, and she was intubated to help her breathe.

"The only injury we noted was the burn where the Taser touched her skin." Dr. Gia pulled the blanket down to reveal the mark.

"Did you see any scars from previous injuries or surgeries?"

"She'd had a c-section."

Eve squeezed Leah's hand. "I'm sorry, sweetie, but we need to take a quick look at your scar."

She nodded to the doctor who pulled the blanket back and shifted the hospital gown just enough to reveal the scar without compromising the injured woman's privacy.

Eve pointed to a spot. "Right here. Do you see that?"

The scar itself was wide and pink. But inside the scar, there were injection marks with small bruises that had formed around them.

Dr. Gia leaned in close enough to see them. "You're right. Wow, that's nearly impossible to see." He carefully counted. "It looks like seven of them. If she was been injected with insulin, it's no wonder she ended up with hypoglycemia."

"But if there are seven injections, that's even more than Mr. Yates," Jenny spoke from near the door. "Why didn't it kill her like it did him?"

Dr. Gia straightened. "Miss Garrity has type two diabetes. That means her body makes more than the normal amount of insulin, but it is somewhat resistant to the effects of the insulin." He looked at his patient. "In this case, her form of diabetes likely saved her life."

They'd need pictures of the injection sites as well as copies of the lab reports. Eve wasn't sure what the procedure for that would be since Leah was currently unconscious.

Dr. Gia carefully rearranged the blanket.

Jenny shook her head as she looked at Leah. "The killer clearly intended to end Miss Garrity's life. We'll need to keep an officer posted around the clock until he's caught. Once he hears that she is still alive, he may try to come by and finish the job."

"It's so horrible. I hope she pulls through." Eve frowned. "What I want to know is whether the owner of the house interrupted the killer, or if the killer assumed she was going to die like Mr. Yates and left without making sure that happened."

"Maybe he thought she was already dead, just like the owner did," Jenny suggested.

"That's possible, too," Eve agreed. Either way, it was a miracle that Leah had survived. "The silver lining in this is that, after seven more injections, the killer likely doesn't have enough insulin left to use on anyone else. At least not based on the contents of the package that was stolen."

If Leah pulled through, would the killer choose someone to replace her? Or did this count as victim number two?

Eve could practically hear the grains of sand falling in the proverbial hourglass.

Chapter Ten

For John, the rest of the drive to Houston was a long one. He'd been worried about Eve, and he was thankful when she called him later to let him know how Leah Garrity was doing and that she'd survived the attack. He prayed that Leah would recover, mostly for her and her daughter but also with the hope that she might be able to give them a description of the person who attacked her so they could make sure he never hurt anyone else.

To help pass the time, he called and spoke to his parents for a few minutes, checked in with Arnold, and then listened to music while he mentally went through the questions he wanted to ask Detective Zeller. Two separate times, he'd lost cell service and had to call someone back again once it'd been restored some distance later.

By the time he fought Houston traffic and arrived at the courthouse, John was more than ready to get out of the car and walk around for a while.

He and Zeller had arranged to meet on the main floor near the coffee stand. John had researched the detective online, seen several pictures, and found it easy to spot him once he entered the room.

Zeller was a short, well-dressed man who was bordering on retirement age. His hair, while gray, was thick and combed perfectly in place.

John greeted him with a handshake. "I appreciate you taking the time to meet with me, Detective."

"You can call me Calvin," the older man assured him. "I'm just sorry you had to drive into Houston. Construction has made everything a mess." He glanced at his watch. "I don't mean to rush you, but I'll need to be back in court in just over half an hour."

"Oh, of course. Can I buy you a cup of coffee?"

Calvin agreed. They got their coffee and then sat at a square table overlooking a courtyard area below. A large fountain with a statue in the middle spouted water that glinted in the sunlight. From this angle, John couldn't quite tell what the statue was.

John took a sip of his overpriced coffee. It was good, but no better than what he could find in Destiny for half the price. "I know we're short on time, so I'll jump right into it. As you know, I'm looking into the Isabelle Perez case. Now, I've read through your case files. I've also spoken with Ms. Perez's college roommate and both of her siblings."

Calvin held up a hand to stop him. "If you've spoken to them recently, then you know more about the case than I do at this point." He took a swig of his coffee, undeterred by how hot it was. "I worked on that case for months and kept it in the back of my mind for several years after that. All I ever ran into were dead ends."

"I understand that. Unfortunately, I've got a murder in my town that is somehow connected to this one." He paused and let that news sink in.

The older man looked doubtful. "After all these years? Are you sure you're not reaching?"

John might have wondered the same if their roles were reversed. "Isabelle's roommate has been targeted by someone who has already murdered one person and is threatening to kill two more times before taking her life. Subtle references have been made to the Perez case, although I admit it could be more of a copycat situation. Still, there's definitely some kind of connection." He tapped the side of his coffee cup. "You mentioned a notebook with thoughts regarding the case. If there's anything at all that might help, I'd sure appreciate it. Even if it's simply an impression of someone you interviewed or a detail that made no sense that might have been left out of the report because it didn't seem related or significant at the time."

When Calvin set his cup down, his expression neutral, John was afraid he might have offended the other detective. After all, being unable to solve a case or put pieces of evidence together was like getting a nasty splinter buried deep in your skin. Always irritating. Sometimes, it came out on its own, but other times, it sat there and festered until you dug it out yourself.

Instead of being angry at the question, Calvin tapped his finger on the table several times, then said, "The strangest thing about the case was the fact that it made no sense. If it weren't for the black rose left behind, I would've been convinced someone had gone into her dorm room by mistake. No boyfriends, ex or otherwise, that might have killed her out of jealousy or spite." He paused in thought. "I tried to find the source of the rose, but that was like looking for a needle in a haystack."

John nodded in understanding. "It's a frustrating case, that's for sure. I've been struggling to connect the murder in my town to what happened to Ms. Perez. There's a possibility that someone knows about the rose detail and is copying that, but my gut says there's a real connection."

The other detective reached into a pocket on the inside of his jacket. He retrieved a battered notebook the size of a note card. "I kept one for every case I worked. Heaven knows why I've held onto them all these years." He lifted the notebook slightly as though testing its weight. "I don't know that anything in here will help you. I kept track of everything, including how often family or friends called for an update. The roommate, Miss Marks, inquired about the case more often than the girl's own parents for the first few years. But everyone has their own way of grieving, and I do my best not to judge." He handed it over then.

"I appreciate it." John tucked it away. "I'll get it back to you after our investigation."

"Keep it. I'd sure appreciate a call if you connect and solve the cases, though. It'd be a relief to know."

"Absolutely. You mentioned you kept track of everyone who asked about the case. Have you been contacted by anyone lately?"

Calvin took a long swig of his coffee. "Other than you? Crickets for probably eight years." He frowned, a hint of sadness in his eyes. "I always felt bad for Miss Marks. She seemed more upset than the victim's parents. I think she blamed herself for her friend's death. Took it personally." He downed the last of his coffee. "I've thought about her from time to time. Is she doing okay?"

John had gotten the impression that she blamed herself as well. He prayed she didn't feel that way anymore. "She's a skilled medical examiner who has done a world of good bringing answers to the families of victims."

A ghost of a smile pulled at the corners of Calvin's mouth. "I'm real glad to hear that. Good for her."

John looked forward to going through the other detective's notebook. He had every intention of reading it cover to cover. But the best resource was sitting right in front of him, and John hoped to take advantage of that while he had it.

"I looked through the case files you sent over, and we noted that you interviewed three different people more than once. What were your reasons for interviewing Miguel Perez and Carl Trevor?"

Calvin rubbed the back of his neck with one hand. "Carl was a janitor at the university. He worked all over campus, but campus security had several complaints originating from Isabelle's dorm. Female students had called in reports stating Carl tended to linger at the restroom doors. Or he would go in to clean the restrooms and not put up a sign letting people know they were being serviced. Sketchy stuff that was never fully proven." He took another drink of his coffee. "He had an alibi for the time of Isabelle's murder. Basically, he was working with another janitor to clean a conference room area, and the other janitor verified it. I brought him in a second time because he just gave off a real creep vibe, but there was nothing I could pin on him, so I had to let him go. It caused enough of a ripple, though, that the university fired him later that week."

John nodded thoughtfully. "I'll see if we can figure out where he is now. If he's in the area..."

Calvin interrupted him. "I'll save you some trouble. He died about five years ago from an overdose. I remember reading about it in the newspaper."

Well, that eliminated a third of John's suspect pool. "What about Isabelle's brother, Miguel?"

"The first interview was done over the phone. He didn't

come into the DFW area like the rest of the family had. I spoke with her parents, and while they were never really suspects, it was clear there were a lot of issues in the home and a lot of animosity between the father and son. I later met with Miguel in person."

"What was your impression of him?"

"Considering his parents, I felt like he was very stable. Successful. I had a limited view of what their homelife might have been, but I felt confident that Miguel's decision to leave as soon as he was old enough had been wise. He seemed to have his life together and was doing well for himself. But he was really torn up about his sister."

John nodded. "I got the same impression myself." Which was why he'd been surprised to see Calvin had interviewed him twice. "Which leads me to the last suspect."

"Jackson Arends." They said the name together.

Calvin finished off his coffee and set the empty cup on the table with a bit more force than necessary. "Jackson had an alibi lined up perfectly. He knew exactly what to say. But the man was slimy. Isabelle and her roommate caught him watching them multiple times. People around campus either never noticed him at all or got a stalker vibe from him."

"But there was never enough to directly connect him to the murder."

"No. We had no motive, no one placing him at the scene of the crime. In the end, we had to let him go."

John regarded the older detective thoughtfully. "You think he did it."

Calvin shrugged. "Without proof, my thoughts mean exactly nothing. But if I were a betting man? Yeah, I would've put it all on Arends. I kept an eye on him until he went to jail. I was glad to have him off the streets.

The man's reaction to interviewing Jackson Arends was not something to easily dismiss. Which meant John needed to look more into Jackson's current whereabouts. "Then you probably know he was released from prison six months ago."

Calvin frowned. "I did *not* know that."

John shared the information about Arends being released and how he'd skipped out on his parole not long after. "The timing between that and everything starting up in Destiny is pretty hard to ignore."

"You aren't wrong. Keep your eyes open. Like I said, the guy has a knack for blending in." Calvin checked his watch and pushed his chair away from the table. "I'm sorry. I know you made a long trip for very little time. If you're still around, I'd be happy to speak to you more when this case wraps up for the day."

"I wish I could, but I'll be heading back shortly." John extended his hand. "I appreciate your time. If anything comes to mind, or if you're contacted by anyone else concerning the case, please let me know. Otherwise, I wish you well."

"Same to you. It'd be nice to finally lay that case to rest."

They shook hands, and then Calvin tossed his empty coffee cup in the trash and crossed the main room toward the elevators.

John took a drink of his own coffee. It wasn't even half gone, and it was still warm enough to make it impossible to gulp. The older detective's ability to tolerate scalding coffee was impressive.

Once back at his car, John opened the notebook that the older detective had given him.

There were notes and first impressions of the murder

scene. Commentary on each person he interviewed. It was a lot to go through, and John had every intention of combing through it, page by page.

For now, the information he'd gleaned directly from Calvin was invaluable.

He started the car, anxious to get back to Destiny. As it was, he'd be lucky to get in before ten.

The first thing John did when he got back onto the highway was to give Arnold a call to update him on the conversation with Detective Zeller. "If we rule out Miguel, I think we're looking for Jackson Arends. But if he's as good at blending in with the surroundings as Zeller says, it's no wonder no one has been able to locate him. The one thing we're missing is a motive behind why he might have killed Isabelle as well as his motive for targeting Eve now."

"I agree. But for now, he's our most likely suspect." Arnold spoke to someone in the background. "Leah Garrity is still in a coma, but the last update from the hospital said she's holding her own. We're all hoping she'll be able to recover. Her family should be arriving late tonight."

"That's good." At least Leah's daughter would soon be with family while she waited for further news on her mom. "I need to call and make sure Eve is set. I think Jenny was going to stay with her at the house once she leaves the precinct."

"You don't need to worry. Chloe invited Eve, Jenny, Megan, Tia, and Paige over after work this evening. They're going to watch a chick flick, eat all kinds of snacks, and fill my house with way too much estrogen." The tone of Arnold's voice said he didn't mind at all.

"With a baby girl on the way, you may as well get used to being outnumbered," John told him with a chuckle.

"You aren't wrong. Tonight, I'll steal some snacks and

lock myself in my office with a video game. Anyway, I'm sure they'll still be here when you get back to town. Swing by, and you and Jenny can work out shifts for watching over Eve."

"Sounds good, Chief. Thanks." Unless Eve objected, he had every intention of being the one to stay and keep an eye on her place.

"Drive safe. We're supposed to get thunderstorms this evening."

"Will do." He'd seen the thunderstorm watch pop up on his phone while he was talking to Zeller earlier. "See you in a few hours." John disconnected the call.

Knowing that Eve was not only surrounded by other people this evening but that she would hopefully be doing something fun, made him feel much more relaxed for the drive back to Destiny.

Even still, the threat against her was hanging like a weight from a frayed piece of rope. John needed to find Jackson Arends—or whoever was responsible for the murder of Yates and the attempted murder of Leah—before he decided it was time to target someone else.

Chapter Eleven

The idea of going back to her place made Eve more than a little nervous, but Jenny had promised to go with her since John was still on his way back from Houston. Then Chloe had invited a bunch of them over to her house for a girls' night out. Eve jumped at the chance to spend time with friends and try to put the case they were working on in the back of her mind for a while.

By the time Eve got to Chief Dolman's, with Jenny driving behind her, the other ladies were already there. Chloe opened the door and ushered them into the living room.

Eve waved at Tia from dispatch and accepted a hug from Paige Wade, who was engaged to Gabe at the station. Megan Keyes, a friend of Gabe and Paige's from high school, stood and welcomed them with a smile. Eve had met Megan a handful of times and knew that she had married Bryce, a firefighter in town, back in November.

Eve's cell phone rang, and she glanced at it to see that it was Anna Perez. "Sorry, guys, this will just take a second.

Anna was wanting to set up a time to meet for coffee over the next day or two."

With the ongoing case, everyone else was aware of who Anna was. Chloe waved at Eve. "Just invite her to come over. I'm sure she could use the company."

"Are you sure?" It was no secret that Chloe preferred smaller gatherings. And she definitely felt more comfortable around people she already knew.

"There's plenty of food."

Even though almost everyone in attendance knew about the case, the women had already made a pact to keep conversation to much happier topics.

Arnold gave his wife a kiss and held up a hand. "I'm going to go hide in my man cave. I hope you all have fun." He turned to Chloe. "Let me know if you need anything." He squeezed her hand and left the room.

Eve wasn't sure whether Anna would want to join them and was pleasantly surprised when the younger woman jumped at the chance.

By the time Anna got there, Paige, Megan, and Chloe had set up an impressive spread on the coffee table in the living room.

Eve brought Anna in and introduced her to everyone. Then she pointed to a large platter filled with candy of just about every kind and color. "I've heard about your candy charcuterie boards. But that's impressive."

Megan grinned. "It's a skill. Besides, Paige would be mad at me if I didn't bring one along."

Paige tossed several peanut M&Ms in her mouth. "Yep." She pointed to the other platter filled with cheese, meat, and crackers. "But what's up with the healthy stuff? That's a new one."

Not that Eve didn't like junk food, but the cheeses looked especially good.

Megan planted her hands on her hips. "Chloe can't just gorge herself on junk food when she's eating for two."

Chloe's cheeks got pink. "I appreciate it. Besides, even though I've never been much of a vegetable person, this baby girl has me craving sugar snap peas. Seriously? Peas?"

Everyone in the room laughed, including Anna who was standing just behind Eve.

"Besides," Megan began, "Bryce made me promise to eat something healthier, too." She patted her flat stomach. "We just found out we're expecting a baby in November."

Paige squealed so loudly that Eve flinched. She watched as the best friends hugged, and then everyone else got a chance to congratulate Megan, too. It was a great way to start the evening together.

Eve released her hair from the ponytail she usually kept it in and quickly braided it down her back to get it out of the way.

They watched a movie, talked and laughed, and ate more food than Eve thought was possible for a group their size.

Anna was super quiet at first, mostly listening and laughing at all the funny comments. But by the end of the movie, she was participating in the conversation as much as anyone else. She and Tia talked quite a bit about their mutual love of home improvement shows.

Eve volunteered to go to the kitchen and get another round of water and sodas. Anna quickly jumped up and offered to help.

In the kitchen, they worked together to collect drinks and place them on a tray to carry back out. The other ladies' voices filtered in through the doorway.

"Thank you for letting me join you all," Anna said as she got three bottles of water out of the fridge and added them to the tray. "This has been so much fun. You're lucky to have so many friends. It's almost like you're a family." There was a longing in her voice that was impossible to miss.

"They *are* pretty amazing," Eve admitted. "You fit right in tonight. I'm glad you decided to come."

"I was so jealous of the friendship you and Isabelle had. Then after..." Anna's voice caught. "I felt so bad. I didn't make much of an effort to see her after you guys went away to college. All that time wasted that I can never get back."

Eve's heart squeezed at the agony in Anna's eyes. "You and Isabelle were sisters. She loved you, and nothing could change that. I promise." She reached out and gave her a hug. "For what it's worth, I always saw Isabelle as a sister. That makes you my little sister by default."

Anna sniffed and quickly wiped away the tears that had escaped and slid down her cheeks. "Really?" her voice sounded strained.

"Yes, really. Who knows? After all these years, maybe we can be friends, too."

"I'd like that." Anna smiled, grabbed a paper towel to blow her nose with, and then washed her hands. She finished helping Eve get the drinks together. "You'll never guess who called me today." She paused. "Miguel. I don't remember the last time I spoke to him."

"That's wonderful!" Eve wondered if John's conversation with him had inspired Miguel to reach out to his sister. "Did the conversation go okay?"

"I think so. It was a little weird. He's married now and has two little boys. I had no idea." Anna's voice caught again. "I'm an aunt."

"I'm happy for you, Anna. I hope this is the start of you guys being in each other's lives."

"I hope so, too." Anna beamed. "I guess we had better get back in there. Sounds like we're missing something hilarious."

Eve listened to the combined laughter of her friends and smiled. "Yeah, I guess we should."

They finished their movie, ate more food, and had fun joking and laughing.

Several of their phones went off with a weather statement. A round of thunderstorms were predicted to roll through Destiny beginning in twenty minutes with a potential for high winds and hail.

A moment later, Megan got a text. She read it, then stood from the couch. "That was Bryce. He's worried about me driving home if the weather gets bad. I'd probably better get going before it hits."

Everyone else agreed. The food was put away in record time while Chloe let her husband know people were going to be heading out soon. He helped carry things out as the storm front's approach brought an increase in wind.

Eve gave Anna a hug. "Don't be a stranger, huh?"

"I won't. Thanks again, Eve." Anna thanked Chloe for her hospitality and took her leave.

"And then there were four," Jenny said as Arnold shut the front door.

Compared to the previous few hours, the house seemed almost too quiet. Especially compared to the sound of the wind whipping the trees outside.

Eve glanced at her watch. "I hope John gets into town soon."

"He should be here any minute," Arnold said.

Jenny nodded. "He's supposed to be coming here first. Then he said he'll follow you back to your place and keep watch overnight. If you're good with that. Otherwise, I'm happy to stay instead." There was a glimmer of humor in her eyes.

"John following me over sounds good. Besides, after this evening, you're probably ready to go home and have a sugar crash." Eve hadn't missed the fact that her friend had remained armed the entire evening. The chief, too, for that matter. Amid all the chaos of the last few days, it'd been nice to relax, have fun, and know they were all safe.

Jenny held up the baggy of candy that Megan had insisted she take with her. "I may need an intervention."

Headlights filtered through the curtains at the front of the house as a car pulled into the driveway. Arnold looked through the window. "That's John right now. Good, you guys will hopefully all get home before this storm hits."

A moment later, he opened the door and waved John in along with a gust of wind.

John shook Arnold's hand, offered smiles to both Chloe and Jenny, and then gave Eve a grin that made her breath catch. It felt as though they hadn't seen each other in days instead of a dozen hours. If it'd been just the two of them, she might have stepped into his arms for a hug. Hopefully, the happy look on his face meant he got some helpful information from Zeller.

"Did everything go okay?"

"I'll fill you in back at your house." Lightning flashed outside. "We'd all better get going."

There was a last quick round of goodbyes. Jenny dashed to her patrol car as soon as the Dolmans shut their front door. She waved and pulled away from the curb.

John walked Eve to her vehicle and waited for her to unlock the door. She turned to look at him before getting in, only then realizing just how closely he stood. Even with the wind whipping around them, the warmth from his chest filled the space between them.

"I'm glad you're back," she said, her voice soft even to her own ears.

"So am I." He laid one hand over hers, where it rested on the handle of the door. He took in her braided hair and, with the other hand, he reached out and started to tuck wayward strands of hair behind her ear. Before he could, the wind whipped them away from his hand. "I missed you." He ran his thumb over the top of her hand.

Without thinking, she turned her hand over. Their fingers entwined as though they had minds of their own. John shifted closer, his gaze darting to her lips.

Another flash of lightning lit up the night sky and was immediately followed by a clap of thunder.

The sound sent a jolt through Eve's body. She crossed her arms in front of her and laughed nervously. "Little known fact about myself. I hate thunder."

"Are you okay to drive home? We could leave your car here and come get it in the morning."

Eve shook her head. "I appreciate that. But we need both vehicles in case we get called in different directions tomorrow." Reluctantly, she turned and got inside.

"I'll be right behind you."

Eve jumped every time thunder rumbled as they drove. She focused on the road, but she could still feel the pressure of John's hand on hers. She wasn't sure what possessed her to respond by holding his hand. It'd been instinct, pure and simple. But he hadn't objected.

What if he had simply been trying to make her feel

better, and she'd misinterpreted it? Warmth flooded her cheeks at the thought. But no, she was almost positive he was going to kiss her until that blasted thunder scared the daylights out of her.

More lightning streaked through the sky, followed by an echo of thunder as she pulled up in front of her place. It hadn't started raining yet, but the air smelled like it was imminent.

She grabbed her things, including a large baggy full of candy, and rushed ahead of John to unlock the door. He was right behind her, his duffel bag over one shoulder. Once inside, he locked the door again.

"Stay here, let me double check the house."

She might have objected last time, but Eve had no intention of doing so tonight. She wanted to know that everything was secure. Thankfully, he returned before long with a definitive nod.

"We're good."

As though the storm had specifically waited for them to get inside, another boom of thunder sounded, immediately followed by the downpour of rain.

John tipped his head toward the living room. "Are you sure you don't mind if I take the couch tonight? I can stay out in my car if you'd prefer."

Eve immediately shook her head. "Don't even think about doing that. You'd be miserable out there in this weather. I appreciate you staying here."

"Of course."

They stood, staring at each other, for a moment or two until Eve cleared her throat. "How'd it go with Detective Zeller?"

John tossed his duffel bag onto the floor next to the couch, set a police radio on the bar, then took a battered notebook out of his pocket. He handed it to her. "Those are all the personal notes he made during his investigation into Isabelle's case."

She leafed through it as she listened to him tell her about the meeting. She was relieved to hear that both Detective Zeller and John felt like Miguel Perez had nothing to do with Isabelle's death.

"Zeller seemed pretty confident that Jackson Arends is the one who killed Isabelle, but he never could prove it. I wish we knew where he was."

Eve handed the notebook back to him and went into the kitchen to put on a pot of coffee. She spoke to him over the island that divided the two rooms. "We should go through that notebook tonight. See if there's anything in there that he forgot to tell you. Didn't he say he kept tabs on him? Maybe there will be a clue in there as to where he might have gone."

She stifled a yawn then, already tired from the day's events.

John nodded his agreement. He must have noticed the yawn because he added, "And you should try and get to bed at a decent time, too. Why don't I have a pizza delivered? That way you don't have to cook anything."

"You won't hear an argument from me."

A gust of wind drove the rain into the windows along the front of the house and pounded on the roof. John had to speak up while placing the pizza order. When he finished, he went to a window and pulled the curtain back. Together, they peered through the darkened pane and marveled at the water flowing down the street. It nearly reached the top of the curb.

"Wow, it's really coming down, isn't it?" Thunder

boomed, and Eve shivered. "We need the rain badly, but I could do without the rest of the storm."

"Same here." He let the curtain fall back into place and turned to face her.

After being outside in all the wind, a small section of hair had come loose from her braid.

John reached over and gently scooped it with one finger and deposited it behind her ear, his finger lingering. "I've always liked your hair," he told her, his voice as soft as his touch. "The braid looks nice. But I think it's especially pretty when you let it flow around your shoulders."

His compliment sent heat right to Eve's face. "Thank you," she whispered.

She reached for her braid, took the band out, and unwound the braid. It tumbled around her shoulders. She combed her fingers through it to bring some semblance of order to the mess.

To her surprise, John threaded the fingers of his right hand through her hair at the base of her neck. "You're beautiful," he murmured, his lips only inches away from hers.

Eve sucked in a breath but didn't move away. Everything about this was complicated. They worked together, and they both had demanding schedules. What she ought to do was take a step back. Regain her senses before things changed too much between them.

But she also wanted him to kiss her more than she'd wanted anything in a long time. She tipped her chin up to look at him, and he took that as an invitation to close the distance between them.

His warm lips slanted over hers, confident and sweet. He put an arm around her waist and drew her closer. It was a good thing he did because she might have melted into a puddle on the floor otherwise. Everything about the kiss was perfect as his warmth surrounded her.

John pulled back a little, a smile on his face as he looked at her appreciatively. "I've wanted to do that for a long—"

Lightning flashed bright enough to startle Eve, closely followed by a clap of thunder that rattled the windows. The lights flickered and went out, immersing them in total darkness.

Chapter Twelve

John pulled a small flashlight from one of his pockets and switched it on. "That lightning strike was close. It probably blew a transformer nearby." He reached for her hand, unwilling to let go of the closeness they'd experienced moments before. Together, they walked to one of the windows. He pulled the curtain back and looked outside. "See, it looks like the whole neighborhood lost power."

"That's a relief," Eve laughed nervously. "I think it's safe to say that I've seen way too many shows where the villain cuts the power to a house before breaking in."

He gave her hand a squeeze. "We're okay. However, if a transformer is out, it might take a while for them to fix it. I'll give the power company a call and report the outage." After closing the curtain, he let go of Eve's hand and searched for the phone number. Unfortunately, the call wouldn't go through. "Looks like the closest cell tower might be out, too." He tried two more numbers, but the results were the same.

He wasn't concerned about the power outage. However,

he would've been worried about being cut off from reaching someone else if it weren't for the fact that he'd brought in his police radio. He retrieved it and turned it on, relieved to hear reports coming through on the main channel. When there was a break, he checked in, letting them know where they were, that power was out in their part of town, and that he was unable to be reached by phone.

Eve worried her lip as she stood and listened to the exchange.

"It sounds like the power outage is only on this side of town. The electrical company already knows about it. We just need to sit tight, and hopefully, they'll have it back on again before long." She gave a tight nod. "Do you have any flashlights or candles?"

"Yes. In the kitchen."

John followed her so that his flashlight illuminated their way. Eve withdrew a large flashlight from the cabinet beneath the sink. Then she got a lighter from a drawer to light a candle on the bar and another on the kitchen table.

"That's a little better," she said. The candles cast harsh shadows on her face. She stopped and listened. "It sounds like the rain has really slowed down. I've got some camping equipment in my closet. There's another flashlight in there, along with a battery-powered lantern." She led the way to her bedroom.

Camping gear? For some reason, that surprised him. "I had no idea you liked to camp." It was one of his favorite pastimes, not that he'd had the opportunity to go very often the last few years. He suddenly pictured the two of them sitting around a campfire and sharing a blanket. The image was so clear he could practically smell the smoke and feel her head resting against his shoulder.

Eve flung the closet door open and started rummaging

around inside with the flashlight. "My family has gone every June for as long as I can remember," she said, her voice slightly muffled from inside the closet. "Here we go."

She stuck her arm out behind her, the lantern in her hand, and he took it. A moment later, she emerged with a second flashlight.

"Nice." John turned the lantern on. It cast enough light that they both flicked off their flashlights. "This will be perfect. And with any luck, the power will be back on before we run out of batteries."

"I hope so."

They'd just reentered the living room when a knock on the front door startled them both. She shifted closer to him, her arm brushing his.

"Pizza!"

John looked at his watch. It was about the time he'd expected it to be delivered. He set the lantern down nearby and peered through the peep hole in the door, Eve's comment about the villain knocking out power before bursting into a home replaying in his mind.

A guy in his twenties stood on the porch. The car's headlights behind him not only illuminated the porch but caught the lightly falling rain in its beams. A restaurant's logo shone brightly on top of the car. John opened the door. "Hey, I didn't know if you'd make it or not."

"I was just down the block. I figured I had your pizza, so I may as well deliver it hot." He pulled a pizza box out of the red insulated sleeve he carried and handed it over. "You have a nice night."

"Same to you." John handed him a tip. "Be careful out there."

The younger man raised a hand in thanks and jogged back to his car.

John closed and locked the door. "Well, at least we have dinner." He held the pizza box out. "Living room or kitchen?"

"Living room. The couch sounds more comfortable."

She led the way, and John followed. He set the pizza on the coffee table. The moment he lifted the lid, the tantalizing scents of pepperoni and cheese filled the air. Eve groaned. "That smells amazing."

John retrieved plates and cans of soda for them to drink, then sat down next to her on the couch. "So you and the other ladies had fun tonight?"

"We did. I know I needed it desperately. I think we all did." She took a bite of her pizza, and then fanned her mouth because the cheese was too hot. She swallowed and took a sip of her soda. "Anna came, too."

"Really?" He hadn't expected that. "How did that happen?"

They ate pizza, and he listened as she told him about her evening. She also told him about Megan's pregnancy announcement and made him promise not to tell another living soul since she wasn't sure whether the news was common knowledge yet or not.

John didn't know Bryce or Megan very well, but he was happy for them.

And he really liked how excited Eve seemed to be. After all the seriousness of the last couple of days, it was nice to see her laugh. Even still, he could tell she was exhausted. What she needed was a good night's sleep. He hoped his presence tonight would make her feel safe enough to sleep in her bed, where she was bound to be more comfortable than lying on the couch.

Eve caught him watching her, and her cheeks grew pink. She flashed him an uncertain smile. Was she thinking about their kiss? He hoped she wasn't having second thoughts. Because if the lights hadn't gone out just then, John had had every intention of kissing her again.

He motioned to a photo on the wall that featured Eve along with an older couple that he assumed were her parents. "You guys seem close."

Eve nodded. "We are. I was sad when they decided to move to Clearwater, but they love it there. They have a house near the river. Dad goes fishing all the time. Mom joins him, relaxes, and reads books. Seriously, it's the perfect way to spend retirement."

"That's nice. Sounds like a good mix of being there for each other and independence."

"Exactly," she said with a nod. "I was one of those kids who wanted to try something for myself, even if it meant failing. My parents encouraged that tendency, for better or worse." She took a drink of her soda. "What about you? You're an only child, too, right?"

"Yep. My parents and I are close as well. I think we have a good relationship. I'm not sure they're quite as independent as your parents are. I'm at the point in my life where I get a lot of hints about finding a nice girl, getting married, and giving them grandkids." John laughed, but his neck warmed at admitting something so personal.

"Oh, if it makes you feel any better, I'm getting that, too. I guess that's what happens when we're the only shot they have at getting those grandbabies."

Eve ducked her chin and focused on peeling a slice of pepperoni from her pizza and popping it into her mouth.

John studied her family photo again. It didn't look like either of her parents had red hair. "So, where did your hair color come from?"

"There are redheads on both sides of my family but not

for a couple of generations. When I was born with bright red hair, it was quite a shock. Now I have a cousin who's ten years younger than I am with red hair, too."

There were a lot of shades of red when it came to hair, but he thought Eve's was the most beautiful. He wondered how likely it would be for her to have a child with red hair. "It's always interesting to see how genetics play out. Was there a reason your parents only had one child?"

"Completely by choice. They only wanted one—always claimed it was so they would outnumber me." She laughed. "How about your parents?"

"They like to tell everyone that I was such a trouble-maker that they knew they'd never be able to handle more than one of me." John grinned at the story. "Truthfully, though, my mom had a lot of health issues, and that led to infertility. It was a miracle she was even able to have me. But there were a lot of advantages to being the only child."

"Do you ever wish you had siblings?"

"All the time. I grew up hoping to have a large family of my own one day." As he said the words, he wondered how Eve felt about that.

She smiled. "I think a large family would be fun." As though she'd just realized what she said, she rushed on to add, "At least it seems like it. I had a friend some years ago who had six siblings. She said being part of a large family meant you either wanted the same for yourself, or it made you join a convent." Her cheeks flushed, and she set her plate on the coffee table. "Do you mind if I take a look at the notebook?"

The sudden change in conversation was obvious, but he didn't mind. They were starting to dive into some personal topics. He didn't blame her for hesitating. "Of course not." He handed it to her.

John finished his pizza as she leafed through the pages, the rest of her slice forgotten. With more than half of the pizza left, she'd have plenty for leftovers the next day or two.

Lightning flashed outside, briefly illuminating the room they were in. Eve glanced at the window nervously, but the thunder that followed was barely audible.

"It looked like there was going to be another round of storms, but they weren't expected to be nearly as severe," he told her, hoping that bit of news would put her at ease. He would have checked the weather report again, but the app wouldn't be working right now.

"That's good." Eve was still nervous.

John set his soda on the coffee table and angled his body to face her. He wanted to reach for her and hold her close. Reassure her that everything was going to be okay. Not just with the weather but the case they were caught up in.

She cleared her throat and looked down at the notebook in her hands. Her hair fell like a curtain, concealing her expression from him.

He was working up the courage to ask if she'd like to go out to dinner with him when this was all over when a horrible crunching noise outside shattered the quiet.

Chapter Thirteen

E ve dropped the notebook she was holding. It bounced off the couch and landed on the floor by her feet. "Is that hail?" At first it sounded like metal colliding with metal, but then it morphed into metal hitting glass. Hit after hit after hit.

John jumped to his feet, a hand on the gun at the small of his back. "No, I don't think so. Please, stay there." He snatched one of the larger flashlights off the coffee table and went to the front of the house to investigate.

He didn't need to tell her twice because Eve felt like she was frozen in place. If it wasn't hail, what was causing that noise? Was someone trying to break into the house? It was hard to tell where exactly the sound was coming from.

John pulled the corner of a curtain back. After a moment, he shined the flashlight through the window. The awful sound of metal and glass crunching stopped abruptly. He stepped away long enough to retrieve his radio and called in.

"This is Detective Paris. I'm still at Eve Marks's house. We've got someone outside vandalizing her vehicle." Eve gasped from behind him as he continued. "The power is still out, so there's no clear visual of the aggressor. Is there a unit nearby?"

Another voice came over the radio. "John, this is Gabe. I'm less than five minutes away. I'm heading in your direction now."

"Acknowledged. Please be advised that the suspect may be running."

"Got it. Switching to channel 3." John did the same. There was a pause, and then Gabe said, "I'm coming in with lights, hoping to catch movement if someone is trying to vacate the area. Hang on."

"Understood." John pulled the curtains back just enough to peer outside.

A minute later, Eve caught the rumble of an approaching vehicle. Only then did she realize she'd been sitting forward, hands clasped so tightly that her fingers were becoming numb. She shook them out and stood.

The radio sounded. "I don't see anyone, but it looks like they did a number on Eve's car. Getting Loki out now to investigate."

"Copy that. I'll meet you out there." John slipped the radio onto his belt and turned toward Eve. There was no missing the agitation on his face. "I'm going to help Gabe clear the area. Lock the door as soon as I go out. Don't open it again until you hear my voice."

"Please be careful."

"Always."

He'd barely left the house before she closed and locked the door behind him. There was no way someone could circle around them and come back to the house without their knowing about it. At least not normally. But with all the lights out, she wasn't taking a chance.

Except for an occasional voice in the distance, Eve couldn't hear a thing. What were they doing? What if the person who did this was the same guy who had been threatening her? What if he was waiting for a chance to take out John or Gabe?

The questions and fear swirled around in her head until her stomach was tied up in knots. What if John got hurt trying to protect her? Or worse? The sound of her heartbeat whooshed in her ears.

"I should've left town," she mumbled to herself.

Ugh! What was taking them so long?

The minutes stretched until it was all Eve could do to keep herself from opening the door and making sure everyone was okay. "Dear God, please protect them."

She jumped when there was finally a knock on the door. "Eve. It's John. Open the door."

Even knowing full well that it was him, she still pulled back the curtain to verify. Relief at seeing them unharmed flowed through her body like water kept trapped behind a dam. She unlatched the door and motioned him inside along with Gabe and his dog, Loki.

She locked the door again and leaned against it. "Did you guys see anyone?"

"Whoever it was, they were long gone by the time I got here." Gabe frowned. "Loki and I tried to track them. He picked up on the scent, but it disappeared once we got to the next street over. Probably got into a car parked there." He pulled a ball out of his pocket and tossed it to Loki, who happily started chewing on it as though it were a giant wad of bubble gum. "It'll be better to take pictures of the damage tomorrow when there's good light. But I called it in and made the report official."

John gave Eve a sympathetic look. "We'll have to

contact your insurance company once the phones are back up. Looks like they took either a baseball bat or a golf club to your car."

"Is it bad?"

"The hood is covered in dents, and both the windshield and driver's window are busted. He left a calling card." John looked frustrated as he lifted a bag in front of him. He was using a tissue to keep from touching the plastic baggy directly. Inside, it looked like another fancy envelope. "We have confirmation that the power outage was thanks to a lightning strike. Which means, whoever did this simply took advantage of the blackout."

Gabe nodded. "It also means that they either live inside the area affected or were watching the house."

"Given the time between when the power went out and the vandalism began, I'm inclined to go with the first option. It was risky, too. If the power had come back on, we might have been able to get a glimpse of who did it." John set his radio back on the bar. "There's a difference between leaving a note unseen and walking right up to your house and causing a disturbance like this."

Eve couldn't take her eyes off the envelope inside the bag. Whoever was after her was getting bolder. More willing to take a risk. It was bad enough to feel like she was being toyed with. But now, she didn't even have her own vehicle. Before, she'd felt inconvenienced. Aggravated. Now, she felt trapped.

She reached into a pocket and pulled out a set of gloves. When she looked up, Eve found both men gaping at her.

"You really do carry them around with you every-where." John chuckled. "I'm not sure whether I should be impressed or worried."

"Both, man. Both are appropriate." Gabe's voice was laced with humor.

"Funny." Eve reached for the plastic bag and held it out so Gabe could take photos of it before she withdrew the envelope. Her name was typed on the outside like the others, and the same type of paper was tucked within it.

John stepped closer and held a flashlight so they could read the typed words out loud.

"It's cute that you think bodyguards will make a difference. They won't stop me when it's your turn."

Eve swallowed hard, then carefully placed the note on top of the envelope. She stepped back and wrapped her arms around her waist, suddenly exhausted. Tears threatened to fall. "Please excuse me for a moment." She grabbed a flashlight off the bar and walked to her bedroom, closing the door behind her.

Eve hadn't been in the room a full minute when the door opened again.

"Eve?" John's voice was soft. Concerned.

She didn't trust herself to speak. Instead, she shook her head and moved farther into the room, hoping he'd take the hint and leave. The light from her flashlight cast an eerie glow as she placed it on her dresser, the beam facing the ceiling.

She could sense John hesitating. Frustrated with herself for being so emotional, she swiped at the stray tears that had found their way down her cheeks.

It must have been all he needed because the next thing she knew, he was standing behind her, his hands on her shoulders. "Talk to me."

"I hate this. All of it," she said, her voice deep with emotion. Frustration built inside her, coiled like a spring that wanted to break free. Never had the four walls of her home felt so much like a prison. "Whoever is doing this—they're obviously after me. If I walk out of here right now and disappear, he'll follow. Then maybe he'll leave everyone else alone."

"Don't even think about it." John's voice came out in a low growl. She turned to face him, surprised by the tone. "Eve, if you try something like that, all you're going to accomplish is putting yourself out in the open. Making yourself vulnerable. This person is not getting his hands on you. Period."

"I know this is your case, John. I know you want to solve it. But if it means no one else dies, then it's worth considering."

"You're right. I have every intention of catching the person responsible and making sure he spends the rest of his life behind bars. If you leave, it's going to make that a whole lot harder to do because I'm going to be out there trying to find you." He softened his voice, his breath warm as it fanned her cheek. "This isn't just about my case. Or solving it. It's about you." He paused, his gaze locked on hers. "Promise me you're not going to leave."

He pinned her with a look that stole the air from her lungs. Intent. Determined.

"John..."

"I'm serious, Eve. Promise me."

"I promi—"

Her reply was swallowed by a kiss that stole every lingering doubt from her mind as his lips covered hers. The kiss was soft at first. Hesitant. But when she placed a hand against his chest and leaned into him, he hooked an arm around her lower back and tugged her closer, deepening it.

Eve had nearly forgotten everything that had happened

that evening until Gabe's voice from the other room broke through their bubble.

"Hey, guys. Look at this. There's something on the back of this envelope."

John broke the kiss he shared with Eve, wishing for all the world that they were a normal couple on a normal date right now. He held her in his arms for another minute before stepping back, allowing his hands to lightly travel the length of her arms before giving them a gentle squeeze and leading the way back to the living room.

Gabe shot him a knowing look and turned to hide his grin.

John pinned him with a stare. "Do you need to check on Paige?"

Gabe and Paige had just gotten engaged and were getting married next month.

"I got a message to her through dispatch. She hasn't been affected by the power outage. She's coming off a long day after being on call once already this week, so she's heading to bed." The smile on his face disappeared. He pointed to the back of the envelope that he must have put back in the bag. "See? Right here."

John watched as Eve leaned in close, using a flashlight to fully illuminate the area. When she stepped back, he looked at the green smudge. It reminded him of a grass stain on the knees of his pants when he was a kid. "It looks like some kind of plant matter."

Eve nodded. "I'm guessing the killer wore gloves when he handled everything since he always does. But maybe something got on them when he was putting the envelope into the bag."

"If all of this was situational with the storm," Gabe began, "then maybe he was in a hurry. With the power out, he didn't realize he'd left anything on the paper."

John turned to look at Eve. "Can the lab test this and figure out what kind of plant this is from?"

"They can. But results won't be quick. It'll take a lot of testing and comparing the information to a database to figure it out. But it's worth a shot."

"Good." John glanced around the dimly lit area. His gaze caught on the open pizza box. "Cold pizza, anyone?"

"Don't mind if I do." Gabe snagged a piece for himself. "I'm going to hang around another twenty minutes or so. Make sure no one comes back." He tipped his head toward Loki, who was asleep on the floor near the couch. His ball lay abandoned near his front paws. "I wouldn't want to wake up sleeping beauty over there."

"Or leave pizza uneaten."

"Or that." Unashamed, Gabe took a large bite of his slice.

As though someone had flipped a switch, the lights flickered back on, ushering in a series of beeps and whirs as the oven and microwave powered up. John blinked against the brightness. "Thank goodness." Having lights on outside would be a huge deterrent.

Eve excused herself to retrieve her phone and call her parents. She then sat on the couch and tucked her legs under her body. The smile on her face when one of her parents answered eased the worry that had been there before.

John and Gabe sat at the kitchen table and pored over

the notebook that Zeller handed over. There wasn't much more than what the detective had already revealed at the meeting. Anything else they found reinforced John's instinct that Jackson Arends was the one they were looking for. How the man seemed to stay off the radar was a mystery.

Gabe nudged John's arm with his elbow, then motioned toward the couch.

Eve must have finished talking to her parents and lain down to relax for a few minutes. She was sound asleep now, her head resting on the arm of the couch.

Gabe jabbed a thumb toward the front door. "I'm going to go walk Loki. I'll check in again before we head out for the night."

"Sounds good." John stood and stretched to work the kinks out of his back. He bent over Eve and touched her gently on the arm. "Eve?" It took another shake before she stirred, opening her eyes and blinking at him. "Let's get you to bed."

She ran a hand over her face and sat up a little. "I didn't realize I'd fallen asleep. I can get back to helping you guys look through the notebook."

He crouched in front of her and touched her cheek with the back of his finger. "You're exhausted. We're done. Gabe is heading home, and I'll be crashing soon, too. So please, Genevieve, do me a favor and go get some sleep."

His words coaxed a smile from her. "My parents are the only ones who ever call me by my full first name."

"Well, it's a beautiful name. And I'm sure your parents would agree you need to get some rest."

She laughed then. "No doubt." She held out a hand, and he helped her to her feet. "Promise you'll wake me if something comes up?"

"I promise." He walked her to the door of her room.

"Sleep well." He pressed a kiss to her cheek. Then, unable to help himself, another to her soft lips.

"Good night." She smiled at him and went into her room, closing the door behind her.

The front door opened then, and Gabe came into the room. "You've got it bad."

"I don't think you're one to talk," John countered, unable to keep a smile from his face.

"And you don't hear me denying it. I'm crazy about Paige." He reached down and absently rubbed Loki's ear. "Take it from me. Time flies, and opportunities come and go. Make sure you grab onto a good thing when you see it."

John might have taken Gabe's words as a tease or even badgered his friend back, but the closeness that Gabe shared with Paige was noticeable. Obviously, Gabe had done something right. "I'll keep that in mind."

"Good. We're going to head out of here. After all the driving you did today, I'll bet you're exhausted. I'll see you tomorrow, yeah?"

"Absolutely. Thanks for your help tonight." John shook his friend's hand.

He saw Gabe and his partner out and gave a wave to the patrol who would be keeping an eye on the house through the night before sitting back down on the couch. He had half a mind to go through the notebook one more time, but his eyes were already aching from exhaustion.

Gabe was right, John really needed to get some rest.

He crashed on the couch and fell asleep immediately. But every time the heater kicked on or the wind gusted, he was immediately awake again. When he did sleep for long, nightmares about losing Eve in the dark of night would drive him toward consciousness.

Around three in the morning, he finally sat up, pulled

up his Bible app on his phone, and read for a half hour. The anxiety that had plagued him all night lessened, and he fell asleep again with a prayer on his lips.

The next morning, John woke at half past six, a good forty-five minutes before the sun would rise. Even though he'd spent most of the night tossing and turning, the last two hours of sleep had been some of the most peaceful he'd had in days. He started a pot of coffee in Eve's kitchen, then showered and changed into fresh clothing that he'd packed in his duffel bag. Then, he took his time going through both personal and work e-mails.

Just after seven, a light rap drew his attention to the front door. He peered out to see Jenny waiting. He ushered her inside.

"Hey," he greeted. "You're out and about early. I've got coffee going. Help yourself. Eve is still in her room, but I heard her alarm go off a few minutes ago."

"Thanks. I wanted to go over the damage to Eve's car as soon as it was light enough. Until then, I brought breakfast burritos." She held up a bag. "I figured you guys could use the pick-me-up this morning."

"Are you kidding? You're a lifesaver."

Jenny dumped the contents of the bag onto the bar. There were four burritos wrapped in foil, along with several containers of salsa.

"Have you eaten yet?"

Jenny shook her head.

John retrieved three plates and poured them each a cup of coffee.

Eve joined them in the kitchen, already dressed in jeans and a long-sleeved black blouse that contrasted with her red hair beautifully. Good morning, guys," she greeted.

John couldn't help but notice that she'd left her hair

down to flow around her shoulders and frame her face. All evidence of her exhaustion from the night before seemed to have been erased. He hoped that meant she'd slept well.

Eve zeroed in on the coffee and food. "Oh, my goodness. I may need to bribe you two to have breakfast ready every morning." She accepted a cup of coffee from him and took a sip, her eyes momentarily closing in bliss. "That's exactly what I needed."

"I'm sorry to hear about your car," Jenny told her. "After we eat, I'll go out and take photos of the damage. Then we'll get it towed somewhere for you."

"I appreciate that."

"And I'll give you a ride to work this morning." John gave her a sympathetic look. "You'll probably have to arrange for a rental through your insurance. It's going to take a while to repair the damage." He hoped her car insurance had good coverage for an incident like this.

Eve nodded, but her shoulders fell a little at the thought. "I'll give them a call when we get to the precinct."

They had nearly finished their breakfast burritos when John's cell phone rang, immediately followed by Eve's. They exchanged looks.

Eve set what was left of her burrito on the table and stood. "That's never good," she muttered as she moved into the living room to answer hers.

John swiped the screen. "Paris here."

The chief's voice sounded from the other end of the line. "We've got a deceased shooting victim at the park on Main."

Chapter Fourteen

The tension in John's car was palpable as he drove across town to Main Street. Chester Park, named after one of Destiny's founding families, was right in the middle of town. It was also one of the largest and most visited parks in the area. During the day, families used the playground, teams played games on the baseball diamond and basketball courts, and people fished along the creek that ran through it.

At night, patrols went by regularly due to the recent increase in drug activity. It wasn't that it was necessarily unsafe, but John wouldn't recommend his friends or family wander through the park alone at night.

He glanced to his right, where Eve was sitting in the passenger seat. She looked straight ahead while her left hand kept twisting the strap of her bag.

John finally reached over and took her hand in his. "Nervous?"

Eve threaded her fingers with his and gave his hand a squeeze. "A little," she admitted. "Now that the suspect has run out of insulin, we don't know how he plans to kill the next victim. Or two, if he doesn't count Leah Garrity." She turned her head to look at him. "Maybe he intercepted another box of insulin. Or had more than one the first time."

"Anything is possible. But according to the different companies we've kept in contact with, that shipment was the only one. Here in Destiny, anyway." Which meant nothing because they weren't even certain of the suspect's identity, much less where all he might have been in recent days or weeks.

He focused his attention on the road in front of them as he gently caressed the top of her thumb with his. Once they pulled into the park, it was easy to spot the crime scene thanks to the caution tape that marked the area off and seemed to offer little deterrence for the onlookers who tried to get as close as they could. Several officers stood between the tape and the crowd to prevent them from entering.

John released Eve's hand and got out of the car, going around to open the door for her. He scanned the crowd, looking for Jackson Arends or anyone else who stood out.

The reporter, Al Crispin, lumbered toward them, his cameraman behind him, trying to keep up. "Can you comment on the scene? Is it true that someone has been shot?" The reporter gasped to catch his breath. "The playground is less than a quarter mile down the path. Do parents need to be concerned for their children's safety?"

"I assure you that this situation has our full attention. An official statement will be released later today." John angled Eve away from the reporter with a hand pressed against her back, and they ducked under the caution tape.

Clint was busy taking photographs of the scene. On the ground nearby, a white sheet covered the shape of a human body.

"A jogger spotted the body almost an hour ago." He

motioned across the way to where a man was speaking to Officer Carrington. The poor witness looked shaken as he pointed in their direction. "He called it in immediately. We barely got here before the news van took up residence as close as they could get."

John positioned himself so he was between the body and the news crew. Thanks to the angle, the cameras would be unable to catch a glimpse. He watched as Eve donned gloves, then crouched and gently lifted the white sheet enough to reveal the victim's head and shoulders.

The woman on the ground looked like she might have been simply sleeping if it weren't for the gray pallor of her skin and her lack of movement. Her eyes were closed, and her dark hair was spread out on the pavement beneath her.

Eve pulled the sheet down farther to reveal a blood-soaked yellow, long-sleeved shirt. But what caught her attention was the way the hands were placed, one on top of the other, over the woman's chest.

"Has this body been moved?"

"She was found like this." Clint motioned to her.

She looked up at John. "It looks like a single gunshot to the chest, and death would've been nearly instant, based on the location of the wound and the amount of blood on the ground. There's no way she would've landed like this. That means the killer was near her. Touched her. I need to get her back for an autopsy to see if we can recover any evidence." She frowned. "Did you find any identification on the scene?"

Carrington shook his head. "Not yet, but there may be something in a back pocket. There's an empty car in the next parking lot over, though. Maybe she came for a walk before going to work?"

John took in her shirt and loose-fitting jeans. Carrington's guess was possible. Something didn't feel right, though, but he couldn't quite pinpoint what it was.

Eve looked up at him. "Do you mind helping me turn her over?"

"Of course not." After pictures were taken, John helped Eve carefully roll the woman to her side.

Eve conducted an exam for several minutes. She found a wallet in one of her back pockets and handed it to John, then nodded for him to ease the woman back to her original position. Eve ran several tests before standing again. John pulled the sheet up over the victim to protect her from the crowd in the parking lot.

"No exit wound. Hopefully, we can retrieve a bullet and run it through ballistics. I see no obvious defensive wounds or possible DNA matter under the fingernails, although I'll do a more thorough search once we get her to the morgue." Eve frowned as she stared at the sheet. "We'll test her clothing to check for gunshot residue, though I suspect she was shot from a distance." She motioned to the wallet. "Who do we have here?"

John opened the wallet. The driver's license was at the front behind a clear plastic protector. "Laney Smith. Address shows she lives here in Destiny. Thirty years old."

It would be up to him to locate and notify her next of kin. He dreaded that part.

He opened the inner compartment of the wallet. "There's at least sixty dollars in here. She wasn't killed as part of a robbery." Gold trim caught his attention, and he pulled a small envelope identical to the larger ones that had been sent to Eve right down to her name printed on the front. He held it out so that she could see it. "I guess that answers the question about whether this murder is connected."

Eve's hand trembled slightly as she reached for the envelope and slid the card out.

"I told you I could get to you anywhere."

A glint of light in the trees to the left caught John's attention. "Eve!" In a heartbeat, his eyes widened as he hooked an arm around her shoulder and jerked her to the side all in one motion.

Pop! Pop!

The sound seemed to echo, making it difficult to tell where it had come from. Immediately, people around them began to yell.

Eve tried to move, but she sagged against him. She held a hand to her side. When she pulled it away again, it was covered with blood.

"No, no, no!" John caught her as her legs gave way. He eased her to the ground as words seemed to float around her.

"We have an active shooter!"

Screams rose from the crowd in the parking lot.

"Someone's been shot!"

"We need an ambulance!"

"Can anyone tell where the shot came from?"

John waved his arm in one direction. "Over there. Back in the trees." He put a hand to Eve's wound and pressed hard, causing her to hiss in pain. They were too out in the open. He needed to get her out of there. "Hold onto me," he told her, then scooped her into his arms and ran, half ducking, until they were behind one of the nearby police cars.

He cupped her face with one hand. "I've got you. Eve! Can you hear me?" Her green eyes shifted to focus on him right before they slid shut.

John had no idea how many times he'd paced back and forth across the waiting room at the hospital. Eve was in surgery, and they anticipated news from the doctor any minute now. As it was, the waiting room was full of people showing their support for one of the kindest members of their team.

Arnold walked past and handed a bottle of water to Chloe. She accepted it with a thankful look as one hand rested on her slightly rounded belly. Arnold sat beside her and put an arm around her shoulders.

Clint motioned to the chair beside him. "You should take a seat, John."

He only shook his head and continued his trek across the room. Every time he stopped or allowed himself to think, he pictured the way Eve had collapsed in his arms. If he hadn't noticed the glint of light reflecting off the scope of a gun in the trees... He couldn't think of what the alternative might have been. Even still, he couldn't get her out of the line of sight fast enough.

As soon as they saw that note left for her, he should have gotten her somewhere safe. Made sure she was out of the shooter's line of sight.

He'd replayed the whole thing in his head more times than he could count. But there'd been no reason to think the shooting victim was connected to Eve's case. He couldn't have known. But he should have.

John glanced at his hands. He'd since washed them, but her blood still stained the cuffs of his shirt. It had felt like an eternity since he pressed against her wound, praying that he could stop the flow of blood long enough for someone to bring her the help she needed. He'd ridden with her to the hospital, then had to watch as they'd wheeled her away on a gurney.

The doctor had been optimistic, assuring them that it

looked like the bullet had missed anything critical, but that they'd know for certain once they took her in to repair the damage.

More than one person congratulated him on saving Eve's life. If he hadn't acted when he did... But right now, John didn't feel like a hero.

All John knew was that he was going to find the person who did this and make sure he never tasted freedom again. Anger fueled his steps. He only stopped moving when the double doors swung open, and the doctor came through.

Arnold stood and came forward. Since Eve didn't have family in town, and her injury pertained to a case, the doctor turned to him with Eve's condition.

"The surgery went well. No major arteries or organs were damaged. If the bullet had hit even half an inch in any direction, my report would be a very different one. To say she's lucky is an understatement. While we will have to keep an eye out for infection, Eve should make a full recovery." He smiled reassuringly.

"That's wonderful news. Thank you, doctor." Arnold shook the doctor's hand. "Were you able to recover the bullet?"

The doctor reached into the pocket of his jacket and held out a small jar. "Indeed. I hope it helps with your investigation."

John finally took that seat next to Clint. He ran his hands through his hair and then clasped them behind his neck as he released a lungful of air. Clint clapped him on the shoulder, then straightened when the chief approached them.

Arnold handed the jar containing the bullet to Clint. "Let's get this to ballistics immediately." He turned his focus to John and gave him a knowing look. "I want you to stay with Eve, make sure no one goes in or out of her room that isn't supposed to be there until I get a rotation drawn up."

"Yes, sir." John stood again.

Somehow, the chief knew that he had to see this through. See that Eve was okay with his own eyes.

The chief spoke with the doctor, who nodded, a grim look on his face, and motioned for John to follow them.

They left the noise of the waiting room behind, went down several halls, and paused in front of room 207. "She may not wake up for another hour or two. Once she does, family will be allowed to visit."

"Her parents are out of town right now. I'm not sure of the details." As far as he was concerned, everyone at the station was her family. He motioned to the door. "Is it all right if I sit in her room? I want to make sure no one unexpected comes in, but I'm also hoping a friendly face might help when she starts to wake up."

The doctor nodded. "That'll be fine. If you have any concerns, you can flag down a nurse or press the call button there by her bed."

John shook the man's hand. "Thank you, doctor. For all you've done."

The doctor gave him a smile and left.

John turned and entered the hospital room. Eve lay on the bed, her face pale, even compared to the white sheets. A blood pressure cuff was wrapped around her left arm while an IV had been placed in her right.

He sat in the chair near the bed and leaned forward, resting his forearms on his knees. "Father, thank You for guiding the hands of the surgeon and for sparing Eve's life. Please touch her and help her body to heal quickly and completely." He let out a steadying breath. "Help us find the person who shot her before anyone else gets hurt."

The image of Eve on the ground, covered in blood, kept coming to mind. The moment she'd lost consciousness, he'd feared the worst. He would never forget how helpless he had felt kneeling beside her, desperately trying to slow the flow of blood and praying that an ambulance would come in time.

He reminded himself that she was safe now, and he had every intention of making sure that remained true.

Light freckles dusted the bridge of her nose, and a few were scattered across her cheeks. Several strands of her pretty red hair rested on one cheek. John reached out and brushed them aside.

She looked so small lying there. It was such a direct contrast to her personality. Eve was always ready to stand up for herself or anyone else that needed it. John appreciated that about her. There was something about her dedication to her job, the kind way she treated others, and those green eyes... He'd been drawn to her since they first met, but only now did he realize he'd been slowly falling for her for a while. It'd taken spending so much time together over the last few days to comprehend just how much she meant to him.

The realization that he might not have had the chance to tell her how he felt hit him hard.

"There are a lot of people out there rallying behind you. Praying for you." Her stillness was unnerving. He took one of her hands in his and covered it with the other. "I love you, Eve, and I need you to wake up."

Chapter Fifteen

A consistent beeping roused Eve from a deep slumber. She couldn't remember the last time she had slept until her alarm clock sounded. Usually, she was awake at least a half hour before it ever went off.

She tried to sit up, but her limbs wouldn't move the way she wanted them to. It felt as though a heavy blanket had been placed over her body.

Why couldn't she move? And why couldn't she open her eyes? She needed to get up and get ready for work.

What started as a pinprick of pain in her side began to radiate outward and intensify. She groaned against it. Memories crowded in.

A body in the park.

Gunshots.

She was bleeding.

Panic pressed against her chest, and she fought to open her eyes. A yell formed in her throat, but before she could scream, a warm hand clasped her own.

"Eve? It's John. You're in the hospital. You're safe."

The voice seemed to float in from somewhere else, but it

was just enough to help anchor her. She tried to open her eyes again, and this time, a sliver of light broke through. It took several more times before she was able to open her eyes and keep them that way.

She followed the hand holding hers up her arm to John sitting in the chair beside her bed. She licked her lips, suddenly realizing how dry her throat was.

John leaned in closer, a relieved smile on his face. "Hey, you. Welcome back." He ran a hand over her forehead. "You had us all worried."

Eve tried to sit up, but her body wouldn't cooperate. "Was anyone else hurt?"

"No one else."

Relieved at the last bit of news, Eve nodded slowly and closed her eyes for several moments. *Thank you, God.* She forced them open again, her eyelids heavy. "Am I okay?"

"You were shot. But they took you into surgery, and the doctor was able to repair the damage. I'm sure he'll give you more details when he makes his rounds, but they expect you to make a full recovery." He smiled at her, though there was no missing the worry in his eyes. "It's just a little hole in your side. Nothing to worry about, right?"

"Right." The corners of her mouth tugged up, and she hoped she was smiling back at him. She licked her lips again.

John brought her hand to his lips and kissed her knuckles. "I should let a nurse know you're waking up. I'll see if they can bring in something for you to drink, too." He studied her face. "You gave me a scare. All of us. I'm glad you're okay, Eve."

He went to the door to flag down a nurse before she had a chance to say anything else. She vaguely remembered him bent over her before blacking out. Had John been the one to get her out of the line of fire? Did they catch the shooter? She had so many more questions that she intended to ask him when he returned.

She didn't get the chance right away, though. Nurses buzzed around her, checking vitals and asking her questions. Eve caught a glimpse of John through the door several times, but he didn't come back inside. Was he standing watch? If so, did that mean the shooter was still out there?

The possibility brought a stab of fear. She was just about to ask a nurse to bring John back in when her phone began to ring from somewhere. She recognized the ringtone as Mom's and craned her neck trying to locate it.

"Hold on, dear." The nurse picked up a plastic bag from the floor by Eve's bed. "We put all of your belongings in here." She fished around for the phone and pulled it out triumphantly. "Here you go."

The screen showed a missed call. It wasn't the first one.

"Did someone tell my parents what happened?"

"I honestly don't know." The nurse looked apologetic. "Do you want me to try and find out for you?"

"No, that's okay. Thank you. I'll just call them back."

"You let me know if you need anything." The nurse patted Eve on the arm and left the room.

Eve stared at the missed call notification a moment before dialing the number. Hopefully, someone else had explained what happened. Her energy was fading quickly, and she didn't know if she'd have it in her to try and tell them the story.

The phone barely rang once when her mom answered. "Eve? Honey, is that you? Oh, we've been so worried about you."

Several clicks followed by an increase in background noise let Eve know they had put the phone on speaker.

Dad's voice came over the connection, strong and in charge. "We're supposed to pull into port tomorrow. As soon as we do, we'll find a flight and head back right away."

Someone had called them, then. Eve wondered who it was. "Please don't, guys, I'm okay."

"Nonsense." Eve could imagine Mom planting her fists on her hips. "You were shot." Her voice broke. "You can't expect us to go on vacationing while you're recovering. When Chief Dolman called and told us what happened..."

Dad continued her train of thought. "We never expected to get a call like this."

"Trust me, I never expected something like this either." Eve yawned, her eyelids growing heavier by the second. The nurses must have put something in her IV for her to be this tired again already.

The door to her room opened, and Eve hoped it might be John coming back. Instead, the doctor came in, a genuine smile on his face.

"Hey, Mom? Dad? The doctor just came in. I'll call you back, okay?"

"We'll be waiting. I love you, sweetheart."

"Love you, Genevieve."

Eve smiled. "I love you both, too." She hung up the phone and turned her attention to the doctor.

"It's wonderful to see you awake, Eve." He looked through the medical chart that the nurses had kept up to date. "Everything is coming along as well as we could expect." He explained her wound and how he was able to repair the damage the bullet had left behind. "If the detective hadn't stepped in and moved you out of the way, your prognosis wouldn't be nearly so positive. I have no doubt that his quick actions saved your life." He smiled kindly. "You will need to keep an eye out for infection, but your road to recovery should be an easy one, considering how very differently things could have ended up."

The doctor's words seeped through the fog in Eve's brain. The look on John's face. The way he'd put an arm around her... He'd tried to get her out of the line of fire, and it could have just as easily been him lying there now. Or worse. She suppressed a shiver and pushed away the memory of the gunshot echoing around her.

"How long will I need to stay here?" She wanted to get out of the hospital as soon as possible. She hadn't spent much time in one, but everyone had told her it was impossible to rest there. Plus, she needed to get back to the morgue so she could get to work on the autopsy. She wanted to see to that herself.

The doctor patted her arm. "I'd like to keep you overnight to make sure you're doing okay, but we should be able to get you out of here in the morning."

She wanted to argue that she was okay now, but with the painkillers they'd given her, she was way too tired to go anywhere. The first order of business was to make sure they weren't putting in her IV again. "I appreciate it."

"Of course. Is there anything that I can get for you?"

"Detective John Paris was right outside earlier. If he's still there, will you please tell him I need to speak with him?"

The doctor smiled, said he would, and on his way out, advised her to get some rest.

A few seconds after the door closed, it opened again, and John peeked around the corner. "Are you okay?"

"Could you flag down a nurse?"

Concern flashed in his eyes. "I'll be right back." He returned a moment later with a nurse and followed her in.

It was all Eve could do to stay awake and focus. She

greeted the nurse with a smile. "I appreciate everything you all are doing for me. But I do have one request. From here on out, I don't want any pain medication administered through my IV that's stronger than extra-strength Tylenol." She pointed to John. "Detective Paris is my witness. Please put the request in my chart."

The nurse's eyes widened. "Of course. I'll add that right away, and I'll make sure everyone at the nurse's station is aware."

"Thank you. I have one more request. My parents are out of town. I'd like to add Chief Arnold Dolman and Detective John Paris as individuals who are allowed to speak to the doctor and have access to my medical information if it becomes necessary?"

"We can do that. Let me go get a form for you to sign."

"Thank you." Eve waited until the nurse left and the door to her room had closed behind her before focusing on John. "The shooter is still out there. Isn't he?"

John dragged a chair up to her bed and sat down. "Yes. There was no sign of the shooter by the time officers headed in that direction."

He reached for her hand. "The doctor dug a .243 out of your side, and Clint took it in to run ballistics. With any luck, we can connect it with another crime in the database."

"The entry wound in the victim's chest looked like it could've been caused by a .243."

"I was thinking the same thing."

Eve stifled a yawn. Her eyelids fell for a moment before she lifted them again. "I want someone to be a liaison between the doctor and my parents." She pulled up her mom's phone number and turned the phone to show John. "I need you to call them. They want to come home and take care of me. But with the shooter still free..." It was getting harder to focus. "Until we know what's going on, they need to stay on this cruise where I know they're safe."

"And you want *me* to call and tell them that?"

"You're the detective on the case. Trust me, my dad is more likely to listen to you than he is to me, anyway."

John looked surprised. "Sure. I'll speak with them." He wrote the phone number down. "You're going to need some time to recover before you go back to work."

"The doctor said I'll make a full recovery and that I should be discharged tomorrow. I will not sit on the sidelines."

When he said nothing, she knew he understood. "I have an autopsy waiting, and it's imperative that I'm the one who does it." Despite every attempt to prevent it, her eyelids slid shut. Even though sleeping was the last thing she wanted to do, the darkness that resulted was more than welcoming. She forced them to open again. "I'm going back to work tomorrow. I need my family to stay far away from Destiny."

"We've got this, Eve. What I need *you* to do is to focus on getting better."

Eve took in a deep breath. Let it out. "John, if you hadn't..." Tears clogged her throat.

He absently rubbed a spot on her arm with his pointer finger. "I never should have had you out in the open like that." He lifted his gaze to her. "He tried to kill you."

Eve tugged on his hand. "Hey. And if it weren't for you, he would have succeeded. You saved my life, John." She yawned again. Sleep was slowly creeping up on her. She pushed it away, but it wasn't going to work for much longer. "Will you stay for a while?"

"Get some rest. I'm not going anywhere." He leaned over and pressed a soft kiss to her lips and another to her forehead.

She let her eyes drift shut. The last thing that went through her mind as sleep claimed her was how safe she felt with John by her side.

John waited until Eve's breathing had evened out before letting go of her hand. He watched her chest rise and fall several times, assuring himself she was okay, and then pulled the blanket up to keep her warm.

"Thank you, God." The prayer came out in a whisper.

He thought over what she said about wanting her parents to stay far away from Destiny right now. He couldn't blame her. It'd be better if she could rest for a few days before returning to work, but she was right. She was the one who needed to perform that autopsy.

John was both immensely proud of her and worried for her. Not just for her safety, because she wasn't wrong: the shooter was still out there. But he was also worried about her health. Going to work too soon could be detrimental to her healing process. It was nearly impossible to argue with her, however, because if their positions were switched, he had no doubt he'd be doing that very same thing.

If she needed him to back her up, then that's exactly what he was going to do.

He left her room and closed the door. After taking a seat in a chair just outside, he dialed the phone number she'd given him.

"Hello?" The poor woman's voice sounded apprehensive. He couldn't blame her. The last time a stranger called, it was the chief to let them know about the shooting.

"Mrs. Marks? This is Detective John Paris. I work with your daughter at the precinct."

There was a shuffling noise, and Mr. Marks' voice came over the phone. "Yes. Genevieve has spoken of you before."

They must have put the phone on speaker.

"Eve's pain medication kicked in, and she's resting now. But she wanted me to reach out so that you wouldn't be worried when she didn't call you herself."

"We appreciate that," Mr. Marks said. "What exactly happened? How was our daughter in a position to be shot in the first place?"

John told them everything that he knew would be in the newspaper tomorrow morning, including how Eve had been investigating a murder and was shot while at the scene. "This is all part of an open investigation. I wish I had more to tell you."

"Is our daughter in danger now?" The question came from Mrs. Marks. There was no accusation in her voice, only worry.

"Until we catch the shooter, we have to assume that she is. That's why Eve needs you to continue your cruise."

Mrs. Marks immediately began to protest, but Mr. Marks' voice overrode hers. "Do you agree with that?"

John nodded even though they couldn't see the movement. "I do. Right now, we don't know why the shooter tried to kill Eve. But the last thing she wants is for that target to shift and include the two of you. We need her focused on getting well and performing the autopsy on the murder victim so we can catch this person before he or she hurts someone else. I'm concerned that she won't be able to do that as well if she's worried about you."

"But who's going to worry about *her*?" Her mother's voice broke.

The question struck John's core. His response was immediate. "Eve and I have worked together for years. I consider her an invaluable colleague and a friend. She was shot right in front of me." The image of her collapsing, blood soaking her shirt, flashed through his mind. "I can promise you that I will not rest until the shooter has been found. I will do everything humanly possible to make sure she stays safe."

He could tell the couple were conversing on the other end of the line, but he couldn't quite hear what they were saying. While John didn't have kids, he could imagine how difficult it would be to be so far away from Eve at a time like this.

"If you really think it's best. We'll stay here for now." Mr. Marks paused. "Will you please keep us updated on our daughter's recovery as well as the progress of the case? Her mother and I will be worried."

"Of course. And I'm sure Eve will call you tomorrow. The doctor hopes to release her first thing in the morning."

"Detective Paris? Chief Dolman told us what you did for Eve. Thank you for your hand in saving her life."

"You're welcome, sir." John swallowed past the lump in his throat. He only wished he'd moved faster or kept Eve out of the line of sight in the first place. There had to have been *something* he could've done to prevent this.

He told her parents goodbye and hung up the phone. They were trusting him with their daughter, and John had every intention of keeping his promise by protecting her life... with his own if necessary.

Chapter Sixteen

Completely exhausted, Eve settled back onto her hospital bed. John had stepped out when a nurse came in to change her bandage and then help her into a set of comfortable clothing that Jenny had brought by the night before. Getting rid of the hospital gown was a relief. But trying to get dressed after being wounded wasn't easy. Every move seemed to pull at the skin around her stitches. That was preferable to being zonked out on pain medication, though.

"Thank you for your help," she told the nurse.

"You're welcome." She waved at the two bouquets of flowers and several balloons that brightened up the room. "I think you're one of my most popular patients. If you need anything else, just call me." With a final smile, the nurse took her leave.

Eve was thankful for such thoughtful friends. The deliveries to her room, along with the visitors she'd had already, made her feel loved and supported. Not once through all of this had she felt alone.

Less than a minute later, John peeked in through the open door and knocked softly. "Is it okay if I come back in?"

"Please."

He entered carrying a paper bag in one hand. "Tia dropped muffins off for us."

"God bless her."

John put a muffin the size of his hand on a paper towel and handed it to Eve. "Looks like blueberry."

"One of my favorites." Eve pinched off a bite and nodded her approval. "So much better than hospital food. Please tell Tia thank you for the contraband if you see her before I do."

John sat in a chair near her hospital bed, holding his own muffin, but there was an expression on his face that she couldn't quite identify.

"What is it?"

He seemed to think through his response. "It's a relief to see you sitting up and alert this morning. Yesterday... was not something I ever want either of us to go through again."

Eve didn't even want to imagine what it would've been like if their positions had been reversed. Waiting. Wondering if he was going to be okay. The thought alone had her stomach in knots. "I'm thankful to be here, too. And I have you to thank for that."

It felt as though there was something else John wanted to say. Instead, he glanced at the door to her hospital room, then brightened considerably. "I have some great news."

"Oh, I could use some of that today. Hit me."

"Leah Garrity woke up from her coma."

"Are you serious? That's amazing!" She grinned, her muffin momentarily forgotten. "Is she doing okay?"

"She's recovering nicely, and she may get to go home tomorrow. Not only that, but she was able to give us a description of the man who attacked her. He intended to kill her, so he didn't attempt to hide his face." John pulled up an image on his phone and showed it to Eve. "We had a sketch artist sit with her, and this is what they came up with."

Eve's eyes widened as she looked at the drawing. "Wow, that's an incredible likeness to Jackson Arends."

He nodded in grim satisfaction. "Not only that, but we showed her a selection of mugshots, and she pointed out Arends' photo without hesitation." He took another bite of his muffin and chewed thoughtfully. "We had an alert out on him already in case he came to town, but now we know for sure that's who we're looking for. We're going to have an officer stay with Leah until we have Arends in custody to make sure he doesn't decide to go back and finish the job."

"That's good. As soon as I get out of here, I'll start on that autopsy. I've already been in touch with Paul, and he has the autopsy room ready."

John set his muffin on the small rolling table nearby and moved to sit next to her on the edge of the bed. "I know you want to get back to work. But will you promise me that, once this is all over, you'll take some time off and give your-self a chance to rest up and heal?"

His concern for her was obvious, and it melted her heart. She smiled and reached out to touch his cheek. He'd changed shirts since last night, but he hadn't shaved. The stubble was rough against her palm. "I promise."

"Good." He leaned in and tenderly kissed her. "If there's one thing the last few days have taught me, it's that we can't always count on tomorrow," he said, his voice just above a whisper. He gently placed a finger under her chin. "You should know that I am hopelessly in love with you. I think I've been headed in that direction for a long time."

His words settled over Eve's heart and warmed her. She couldn't have stopped her smile if she'd tried. She placed a hand against his chest and felt his heart beating against her palm. "I'm relieved to hear that, Detective. Because I love you, too."

John grinned, then gently curled an arm around her before kissing her again.

Eve had just settled into the comfort of his arms when someone cleared their throat from the doorway. She'd forgotten all about the hospital and the case. For a few minutes, nothing existed for her except John and the newfound love they were just beginning to understand.

With a chuckle, John leaned back and turned to face the door.

The nurse stood in the doorway holding a vase filled with six red roses. "I'm sorry to interrupt, but you got another delivery, Eve." She smiled and stepped forward. "You may have to rent a separate car just to get all these home by the time you leave," she teased as she handed them over.

"Thank you so much, Sherry. They're beautiful." Eve took an appreciative whiff of the beautiful red blooms as the nurse left the room again. "I wonder who they're from." She took the tiny white envelope off the stick nestled in the bouquet and took the card out.

The moment she read the words, the vase slid from her grasp. John barely caught it before it fell to the floor.

"Eve, what hap..." he stopped when he saw her face. Immediately, he moved to stand beside the head of the bed and read over her shoulder.

"They were all out of black roses. You won't be so lucky next time."

He took the card from her and took his radio off his belt.

Eve barely heard him alert the others of the incident.

"I need Logan to track these flowers down right away. And I want all deliveries to Leah Garrity inspected completely before she receives them." He glanced at Eve. "We're gonna find this guy."

John escorted Eve, a protective hand against her back, through the halls of the precinct to the far side where the morgue was located. He originally suggested driving her to the ambulance bay, where the bodies were brought in. It would have saved her a great deal of walking, but she insisted on going in through the front as though nothing had changed.

Several of their colleagues welcomed her back with hugs or vocal gratitude for her safety. She put up a good facade as they made their way to her office. She couldn't fool him, though. He'd taken a bullet in the past. He knew just how much it hurt and how much being active so soon could drain a person, especially when all she'd taken today were over-the-counter painkillers.

That said, he also knew that if someone could power through this, it was Eve.

They entered the morgue, and Paul hurried over. "Dr. Marks, it's good to see you. I'm glad that you're okay." He gave John a nod. "I've got the autopsy room ready to go. Let me prep Miss Smith, and I'll let you know when we're ready." With that, he rushed off.

As soon as they entered her office, Eve's shoulders dropped a little. John helped her to the desk chair where she eased herself into it with a groan.

"You need to be careful not to overdo it," he warned,

earning him an exasperated look from Eve. He volleyed one right back at her. "I've been shot, Eve. Trust me, I'm speaking from experience. You can fake it all you want, but I know exactly how you're feeling right now."

Eve leaned her head against the back of the desk chair and let her eyes close for a few moments. "How did I not know this? Was that before you came to this precinct?"

"I worked in San Antonio for a few years. I'd be lying if I said getting shot didn't play into my decision to come back home and work here." His injury hadn't been much more serious than Eve's, but he remembered the burning and pain. He'd been fortunate that the bullet in the shoulder hadn't damaged anything major. Still, recovery hadn't been easy. Thankfully, Eve wouldn't need months of physical therapy like he had. John rubbed the scar through his shirt. "All I'm saying is that you don't need to pretend. At least not around me. If you need help, ask for it. We're in this together."

"I appreciate that." She opened her eyes and looked at him. "I appreciate *you*." She reached out, and he took her hand. "I'm beginning to think your suggestion to take a few days off was right on the money." She chuckled, then groaned. "Oh, laughing hurts."

"So will sneezing and coughing, FYI."

"Fun. I appreciate the heads-up." She shifted her weight slightly and gingerly pressed her hand to her side. "So where are you headed now?"

"I'm going to check in with everyone. Logan is trying to tie the flowers to Jackson. Plus, his photo is everywhere. Someone has to have seen him. We'll keep checking the tip line. And that bouquet was ordered from somewhere in town, and we're going to figure out where that is. The ballistics report should be back soon, too." He gave her hand a squeeze. "Let me know as soon as you're done, and I'll come get you. We can update each other on anything that might be useful."

Eve nodded her agreement. She looked as apprehensive about him leaving as he felt. But Carrington was guarding the door to the morgue, every office in the building was on high alert, and John could do a lot more working directly on the case.

Still holding Eve's hand, he offered up a prayer. "Heavenly Father, we ask that you be with each of us as we try to piece this case together. Give us the wisdom we need to find Jackson Arends before he hurts anyone else. I pray for protection over Eve. Keep her safe. In your Son's name, we pray. Amen."

"Amen," Eve echoed.

"I'll see you in a while." He bent down and pressed a kiss to her cheek. "Be careful."

Reluctantly, he let go of her hand and headed out.

At the door, he passed by Carrington, who wouldn't allow anyone to pass who wasn't supposed to be in the morgue.

As soon as he entered the bullpen, where many of the officers worked at their desks, Clint stood and strode to him.

"Ballistics came in. Unfortunately, the bullet doesn't match anything else in the system. Looks like it was shot from your run-of-the-mill hunting rifle."

"Meaning half the households in town could have one."

"Yep. And if it's an older rifle, it may not even be registered." Clint looked disappointed. "Sorry, man. I was hoping for better news. How's Eve doing?"

"She's working with Paul and starting the autopsy now."

"That's good. I sure wish she hadn't had to come in, though."

"You and me both. But you know how she is. Nothing keeps her down." He motioned to the door leading across the hall. "Have you heard from Logan yet?"

"I was about to head that way to check in with him."

Eve leaned against the autopsy table. The acetaminophen she'd taken for pain had seemed to help when she first left the hospital. Right now, she doubted it was doing a thing as a deep ache radiated from her wound, accompanied by a burning pain. She had to focus. They needed to get that bullet, and then she could sit down for a while and let Paul finish the autopsy. He'd been asking to take point on one, anyway, and she knew he was ready.

They'd already found an interesting piece of evidence on Laney Smith's clothing that she had Paul run to the lab immediately. It was a piece of a wilted flower petal, and it looked like it'd landed on Laney's shirt where the blood had prevented it from falling off or blowing away.

Eve didn't recall seeing any purple blooms in the vicinity of the crime scene.

Of course, there was a chance the petal may have been deposited by the wind. She had a feeling there was more to it than that and hoped it wasn't just wishful thinking.

They'd already run a full-body x-ray and had determined the location of the bullet. Eve took in a deep breath, tried to push the pain to the back of her mind, and began the process of retrieving the important piece of evidence.

She caught Paul casting worried looks in her direction

several times and realized that she wasn't talking to the deceased like she normally did.

"Can I get you anything, Dr. Marks? You're looking a little pale. I can finish that if you'd like."

"Thank you, Paul, but I've almost got it. If you don't mind, though, could you wheel my desk chair in here, please?"

He agreed and returned with it momentarily.

Eve reached into the body and, with the help of a small pair of forceps, she was able to grasp the bullet and pull it out. "There we go."

The bullet was a .243. The same caliber that had landed her in the hospital. Satisfied, she dropped it into the jar she had waiting, and screwed on the lid. "If you'll run this to the lab, I believe I'll take you up on the offer to finish the autopsy."

"Yes, ma'am." Paul took the jar and jogged out of the room.

Eve eased herself into her chair and bit back a cry of pain. On second thought, as soon as they got this autopsy wrapped up, she had every intention of filling the pain medication prescription the doctor had sent home with her.

When Paul returned, he continued with the autopsy as Eve observed. He needed little guidance, and since the cause of death wasn't in question, they were able to wrap it up by the two-hour mark.

Paul was just about to take the body back to refrigeration when Katie, one of the techs in the lab, strode in.

"Hey, I've got an ID on that flower petal you found. It's a Texas mountain laurel. I thought I recognized it. They only bloom for a few weeks every year, and we're right in the middle of that time frame here. But," Katie held up a finger, "here's where things get interesting. Do you remember that green smudge on the note you received after someone tore into your car?"

At Eve's nod, Katie continued. "The source was a lot more difficult to identify, but it's also from the same type of plant." She handed a printed report over.

Eve's mind raced as she scanned the information. The petal alone didn't necessarily mean anything. It could have come from anywhere. But they knew that the smudge on the note was placed there by Jackson Arends when he got the note ready. Together, the evidence was impossible to ignore.

"This is super helpful, Katie. Thank you so much."

The tech grinned before leaving the morgue.

Eve dialed John's number. He picked up after the first ring. "Hey, I've got something for you."

"What a coincidence. I was just coming to see you." John's voice grew louder as he strode into the room. He hung up the phone and slid it into his pocket. "We found something, too." He stopped in front of the chair where she was still sitting.

She motioned for him to go first.

"The flowers that were sent to you came from the hospital's gift shop. The order was called in and paid for over the phone. With a credit card."

Eve's brows rose.

John continued. "The credit card is owned by a Melissa Brown. She lives on your street, and we think the card was stolen from her mailbox and activated solely for the purchase of the flowers." He shifted to one side so Paul could roll the gurney past them. "It turns out that Leonard and Melissa Brown are away on vacation right now. It would have been easy to go through their mail if they didn't have it held at the post office."

"But why, after going to such great lengths to stay invisible, did Jackson use a credit card?"

"He's getting desperate, Eve. You were supposed to die out there. He was probably afraid to step foot in the hospital, but he wanted to get to you somehow."

Eve shivered, suddenly cold. She crossed her arms in front of her. "Well, we found a flower petal on the victim when we started the autopsy." She told him where it came from and how the smear on the note was a match to the same kind of plant. "I'm surprised I didn't recognize it myself. They produce such pretty purple blooms..." She stopped as the pieces came together.

She pushed against the chair to stand, but the moment she did, her heart pounded in her ears, and darkness started to close in.

The next thing she knew, John was cradling her on the ground, his brows drawn together. His fingers lightly caressed her cheek. "Can you hear me, Eve?"

"What happened?"

"You blacked out for about thirty seconds." He touched her forehead with the back of his hand. "You're really pale. How are you feeling right now?"

She wanted to tell him she was fine, but he'd know she was lying. "Lightheaded," she admitted. When she tried to sit up, the room spun around her. "Yeah, that's not going to work."

"Okay, I'm getting you back to the hospital."

"That's not necessary, John. I just need a minute."

He pierced her with a look that told her there was no use in arguing. "I can take you, or you can go by ambulance. The choice is yours."

She gave him a single nod, and he called someone on his phone.

"Clint, it's John. I need to get Eve back to the hospital. Can you meet me around behind the morgue with a car, please? Yep. Just let me know when you're here. Thanks."

Eve shut her eyes, but it didn't stop the spinning feeling. She took in deep breaths, willing it to slow before she started to feel sick. Suddenly, their conversation before she passed out came back to her.

"Oh!" She patted his arm several times in urgency. "The flower. John, it's a Texas mountain laurel. I should've known because there's one just across and down the street from my house. How much do you want to bet that's where the Browns live?"

"And he's likely hiding there since the Browns are out of town." John got a text that must have been from Clint letting him know he'd arrived. He stood and lifted Eve into his arms. "He could keep an eye on you. Easily get to your house. If he'd been going back and forth regularly, Loki might not have been able to track him."

He carried her to the loading doors as they swung open. Clint was on the other side, ready to help John ease Eve into the passenger side of the car.

Eve grunted with the effort as she settled into the seat. "And that's why he showed up at the house when the power went out. It went out at the house he was staying at, too. He looked out, saw the whole neighborhood was dark, and couldn't pass up the opportunity."

John reached across her to buckle the seat belt. "He might still be there."

Clint tossed him the keys to the car. "What am I missing?"

"I want you to go by the Brown's home without being seen." He gave him the details. "Verify that there's a Texas mountain laurel in the front yard. If so, call it in. We'll get a team together and go in. We think might be where Jackson is holed up."

Chapter Seventeen

John hated taking Eve to the hospital and then leaving her there. He'd made sure Carrington followed them over, and the officer wasn't going to let her out of his sight. As much as John wanted to stay and make sure she was okay, he needed to catch Jackson Arends. Because the truth was, she would never be safe until the serial killer was behind bars.

Clint verified that the Brown home did have a Texas mountain laurel in the front yard. It was large and situated right against the house near the porch. If Jackson were going in and out of the home at night, he could easily brush up against the bush.

Now John stood at the ready in his tactical gear, handgun drawn, outside the front door.

"This is the Destiny Police Department. Jackson Arends, open the door."

There was no response.

In seconds, they breached the front door. Noise coming from the other side of the house told them that Clint's team had successfully breached the back door as well.

"Is there anyone in the house? This is the Destiny Police Department." John's voice filled the living room. "Jackson Arends, I need you to come out with your hands on the back of your head."

The house remained eerily quiet.

"All right, let's clear the house."

Together, the teams went room by room until it was confirmed that the house was empty.

"Detective." Jenny's voice came from a front bedroom. "You need to take a look at this."

John walked in and stopped in his tracks. The room itself was small and sparsely decorated with a full-sized bed, a dresser along one wall, and a chair against the other. The Browns most likely used it as a guest bedroom.

Which was why the photographs on the wall were so startling. Four-by-six-inch photos of Jackson's victims had been taped haphazardly to the white paint. Yates on the couch in his apartment. Leah Garrity on the floor in her employer's home. A close image of Laney Smith dead in the park. And then there were newspaper clippings and photos from Isabelle's case.

Photographs of Eve took up another section of the wall. Jackson had taken pictures of her going into her house, getting in her car, walking into work, and there was even one showing John and Eve heading into the Corner Café for breakfast the other morning.

"Check this out. This guy has a whole setup here." Clint stood in front of a card table that had been situated in front of the window. The entire surface of the table was covered. Apart from a laptop and small photo printer, everything else appeared to be old food wrappers and empty drink containers.

John approached the window, and with the end of his pen,

he pulled down one of the blind slats. Eve's house could clearly be seen across and down the street. Anger boiled as he took in the disheveled quilt on the bed. "Jackson was living here. There's no way he didn't leave prints. I want the entire place processed." He was satisfied to see everyone jump into action.

Clint walked over to stand with John. "If Jackson isn't here, then where is he?"

John scanned the photos on the wall. Jackson had followed Eve everywhere. Which meant he probably knew where she was now. "The hospital."

The last place Eve wanted to be was back in the hospital. Since she'd just checked out a few hours ago, and given the nature of her injury, she was fast-tracked through triage. Thanks to Carrington, she was already in a private room. He had claimed a spot outside where he vetted everyone before they came in.

Now Eve was in a hospital bed while a nurse she hadn't met before worked to get an IV in her arm. The nurse, who looked to be in her sixties, took an alcohol swab from the metal tray resting on the small rolling table and cleaned Eve's arm. Then, she expertly got an IV started.

"There we go, honey. We're going to get you started on some fluids to help since it looks like you may be a little dehydrated." She patted Eve's arm. "Can I get you a warm blanket?"

"Yes, please." She'd felt chilled ever since passing out at the morgue.

When the nurse said the blanket was warm, she wasn't kidding. Eve couldn't contain the sigh of contentment as the heat seeped through her clothing and began to bring relief to her cold limbs.

"Now, when was the last time you ate something?"

Eve thought back over the day and realized with a start that she hadn't had a thing since the blueberry muffins that morning. And here it was, nearly six in the evening. She told the nurse as much.

The nurse shook her head with disapproval and looked at the clock on the wall. "I'm going to call down to the cafeteria and have dinner brought up for you. In the meantime, I'll get some saline going in your IV. Then we'll take some blood and run a few tests. Make sure there's nothing to be concerned about." She looked at the monitor. "Your blood pressure and heart rate are a little high, but if you're in pain, that's normal. Okay, hang in there, and I'll be back in just a bit."

Once the nurse had done what she said, she patted Eve on the arm again and headed out of the room, leaving the metal tray and trash on the table.

Eve had refused extra pain medication when they first brought her in. She wanted to be awake and aware when they got a report about the Brown's home. What if Jackson was inside, waiting for the officers? Eve prayed that John and the rest of the team stayed safe as they went to investigate.

Exhausted, she closed her eyes for a few minutes. She focused her attention on the weight and warmth of the blanket and tried her best to ignore the pain in her side.

The squeak of a cart in the hall pulled Eve back to consciousness. Apparently, she'd fallen asleep, although judging by the liquid level in the saline bag, it hadn't been for long.

Carrington moved to the doorway. "Eve, your food is here. Are you ready for it?"

"Yes, thank you. Have you heard anything about John?" Now that Eve was still and inactive, she realized just how hungry she really was. She pushed herself to sit straight.

Whatever they'd sent from the cafeteria, she hoped it was edible.

"Nothing yet." There was a shuffling sound. "Here, I can take it in to her—"

His words were cut off by the unmistakable sound of a Taser. Eve's head jerked up in time to see Jackson shove Carrington backward into her hospital room, the Taser pressed against the man's side. Carrington crumpled to the ground.

Jackson leered at her as he kicked the door shut behind him. Without turning, he locked it. He grabbed the stand containing the patient monitor and knocked it down before shoving it up against the door as a barricade.

In the process, the tubing that ran from the monitor to the blood pressure cuff around her arm popped off.

Eve threw the blanket off her and got out of her hospital bed, pain pulling at her side in protest. She shuffled around so the bed was between herself and Jackson.

He laughed. "You think that's going to stop me?" He pulled a knife from his waistband and held it up, the blade glinting beneath the lights overhead.

With the other hand, he shoved the rolling bed toward Eve. It collided with the side where she'd been shot and knocked her to the ground.

Ignoring the pain, she got to her feet as he rounded the bed, the knife raised. A sneer contorted the man's face, making him look like some kind of monster. "You've had this coming for years. You and your friend thought you were so much better than everyone else. Walking around campus with your noses in the air." He slowly rounded the bed as he raised the knife. "I let it go until that article came out. You've got people fooled into thinking you're some kind of hero."

"I'm not a hero. I never claimed to be." Eve shuffled around to keep the bed between them. "I'm part of a team. We rely on each other. Work together. Any success I have is thanks, in part, to what they contribute. I couldn't do any of this without them."

Jackson stood up straight. "All your group has done is run around like chickens with their heads cut off until I fed you a clue." His head tilted slightly as he looked at her. "And when all of this is over, they'll know you're the one who lost."

"You're not making it out of here alive, Jackson. Not if you kill me." She glanced over at Carrington, relieved to see the officer was breathing even if he was still unconscious.

"We'll see about that." He put a hand on the bed, and it looked like he was ready to shove it toward her again.

"What are you going to do? You've got nothing left, Jackson. A team is over at the Brown's place right now. That's where you've been staying, isn't it?"

Surprise flashed in Jackson's eyes, quickly followed by disbelief that morphed into anger. He shoved the bed hard, knocking her backward into the wall. She reached for the metal tray on the rolling table and held it with both hands as Jackson rounded the bed. He held the knife high and brought it down. Eve used the tray to block it. The collision sent vibrations through the tray, and pain shot through her system like a bolt of electricity.

This time, when Jackson approached, Eve blocked the strike again and followed it with a knee to the groin.

Unfortunately, it wasn't hard enough in her weakened state.

He howled in anger. "I'm really going to enjoy killing you," he snarled.

Someone pounded on the door to the hospital room. "Eve!" The sound of John's voice on the other side gave Eve the push she needed.

Momentarily distracted by the sound of someone trying to kick the door in, Jackson's gaze darted in that direction. Eve took several large steps forward, holding the metal tray in her hands like a baseball bat, and swung with all her might. The tray collided with the side of Jackson's head.

Eve felt the stitches in her side tear with the motion, the pain bringing her to her knees.

Jackson growled, and when he turned back around, blood trickled from his temple down his left cheek. Without a word, he pivoted and lunged Eve, the knife raised again.

Eve scrambled to get the tray positioned in front of her to block the blow when the hospital room opened. The equipment on the floor was easily shoved aside as John and Jenny entered, their weapons drawn.

Jackson rushed Eve and grabbed her by the shoulder, keeping her on her knees on the floor. He held the knife to her throat and turned to face the officers defiantly.

"Police! Drop the knife and put your hands in the air!" John didn't take his eyes off Jackson.

"I'll kill her if you—"

The deafening sound of a gunshot filled the small room, followed by a thud as Jackson slumped to the ground, a single gunshot to his chest. The knife landed on the floor next to Eve's leg.

Air whooshed from her lungs as she fell to her knees on the floor.

John kicked the knife away, then knelt beside Eve, concern etched into his features. He placed a hand against her side where blood was starting to seep into her shirt. "Did he cut you?"

"No." Eve shook her head. "I think I ripped my stitches fighting back."

Jenny bent over Jackson and checked for a pulse. "He's gone." Then she moved to Carrington, who was starting to groan from his spot on the floor.

Several other officers flooded the room followed by emergency medical staff.

John eased Eve to her feet, then held her close. "It's over," he murmured next to her ear.

Over. Not just the nightmare of the last few days but the emotional turmoil that had followed Isabelle's death. Eve's eyes flooded with tears. Her best friend finally got the justice she deserved. "Thank you, God, for bringing us through this," she prayed as she wiped the tears from her eyes.

The nurse who had been helping her earlier rushed in and took one look at the blood on Eve's shirt. "Oh, dear. Come on. Let's get you back up on the bed and see what's going on."

Without hesitation, John scooped her into his arms and followed the nurse to another room before gently setting Eve on the bed.

Eve flinched as the nurse examined her wound and cleaned away the blood.

"I'll want the doctor to take a look at it, but I think we can close this back up again." She looked at Eve over the top of her glasses. "When we release you this time, I expect you to go home. Stay hydrated, eat, and rest."

"Yes, ma'am." Eve looked forward to doing exactly that.

John squeezed her arm. "So she's going to be okay?"

"Again, the doctor will have the final say. But we probably don't need to keep her overnight."

John nodded his thanks, then leaned over to rest his head against Eve's. "I want to stay here with you. But since I'm the one who shot Jackson, I need to get back to the station. There are procedures to follow."

"Okay." Eve leaned into him.

There were so many things she wanted to say. To thank him for saving her life again. Ask if he was going to be okay and what was going to happen next. But it was too much right now, and he must have sensed that, because he cupped her cheek in his hand.

"I know. I'll find you as soon as I can."

John hated not staying at the hospital with Eve. But even though there was no question that his use of force against Jackson was justified, there were procedures to follow, statements to give, and numerous steps to go through.

It took longer than he wanted, but he was thankful that Jenny messaged him from the hospital to let him know the doctor had given Eve the green light to go home, and that Jenny would drive her there.

By the time he finished everything and was able to drive over to Eve's house, he was surprised to see numerous cars parked out front. He approached the door as it opened, and Jenny waved him inside with a grin.

He took in the small crowd of people in Eve's living room and kitchen. Pizza boxes were open and set up on the bar. Lively country music played from somewhere in the house.

John scanned the room until he spotted Eve sitting on the couch surrounded by a variety of people, from officers to the techs she worked with. She was laughing at something, her eyes twinkling.

He'd always considered the people he worked with at the station to be his extended family. And this, right here, was exactly why.

"Thank you, Lord, for your mercies today," he whispered.

Eve looked up and saw him, and a smile lit up her face.

"Hey, you." She motioned him over. "I'm glad you made it. There's pizza. Sodas are in a big cooler in the kitchen." Her brows drew together a little. "Did everything go okay?"

John might have sat next to her, except there was no room on the couch right now. "Yeah, it was fine. If I'd known you all were having a party, I might have just skipped all that pesky paperwork."

That earned him several laughs from around the room. Fellow officers shook his hand, congratulated him on a job well done, and someone shoved a plate full of pepperoni pizza toward him.

"I hope this was okay," Jenny said, her voice low. "I figured she could use the distraction."

"Are you kidding? You're a genius. Thank you."

"You're welcome." Jenny flashed him a smile. "Oh! Look who else is here." She pointed across the room to where Anna Perez stood talking to someone John didn't recognize. "They showed up at the hospital, so I invited them to join us. Come on. They were hoping to talk to you." She led the way.

As they neared, the man next to Anna turned, and there was no missing the family resemblance.

Anna smiled. "Detective Paris, it's good to see you

again. I wanted to officially introduce you to my brother, Miguel."

The men shook hands.

"I can't thank you enough, Detective, for bringing some much-needed peace to our family." Miguel put an arm around his little sister's shoulders. "Not just when it comes to stopping Isabelle's killer, but your hand in helping me reconnect with Anna."

Anna looked up at him. "I'm moving to Corpus Christi. We're selling the house—something I should have done a long time ago. I'm looking forward to being near family. I have a couple of nephews I need to spoil and some lost time to make up for." She gave her brother a pointed look, but he only chuckled in response.

John liked that Anna would no longer be alone. "I'm happy for you both. I hope you'll stay in touch with Eve. I know she'd like that."

"Most definitely." Anna nodded and glanced toward Eve.

John saw someone approach and turned to see Carrington with a sheepish look on his face. Anna and Miguel moved away, giving them a moment to talk.

"I'm sorry. Someone was approaching Eve's room. While I was checking her ID, Jackson must have come from the opposite direction."

John put up a hand to stop him. "You couldn't have known. I'm just glad you're okay."

"Me, too." Carrington ran a hand through his hair and nodded toward Eve. "She's one tough cookie, isn't she?"

"She sure is."

John ate pizza, visited with friends, and enjoyed watching Eve. Occasionally, she'd raise her gaze to his, and it made him wonder if she was looking forward to talking to him as much as he was her.

Finally, someone got up from the couch, and John took the spot right next to her. "You're a popular woman tonight." He nudged his arm against hers.

Eve chuckled. "I'm pretty sure it's the food. The last few days have been stressful for everyone."

"I'm sure the food is a bonus. But I'm confident it's all you, sweetheart. I can only speak for myself, but I've found it's impossible to stay away from you."

"Oh, yeah?"

"I'm considering asking the chief if I can move my office into the morgue."

Eve tipped her head back and laughed. "I'm sure he'll be quick to approve that request."

John set his plate on the coffee table and turned toward Eve. "Now that all of this is over, I thought maybe I could take you out on a real date. We could go somewhere nice, revel in the fact that we don't have to worry about a deranged serial killer, and enjoy some good food."

Several people nearby had tuned in to their conversation, their expressions curious.

"You know, without all of these people milling around." He reached for her hand. "What do you say, Eve?"

"Absolutely."

John couldn't have cared less who was watching when he leaned forward to press a kiss to Eve's lips.

The room erupted in cheers, clapping, and more than one catcall.

Epilogue
Two Months Later

John stared into the campfire and watched as the flames gently licked at the marshmallow he was toasting. Just when the sugar puff was about to burn, he pulled it out of the heat.

"Perfect," he announced with satisfaction and held it up for Eve to see.

Every side of the marshmallow was toasted brown. He sandwiched it between two graham crackers along with a square of chocolate and took a bite.

"Mmmmm." *So good.*

Eve, who was sitting in a camp chair next to his, chuckled at him. "How many of those have you eaten?"

He held up three fingers. "This is definitely the last one, though." He smiled across the fire where Eve's parents, Carlton and Gemma, were sitting beside each other. "I couldn't possibly eat another bite now, not after that amazing pocket stew."

Carlton had chopped up potatoes, carrots, and onion then combined that with a hamburger patty before seasoning and wrapping it in foil. The packets were placed in the fire where they had cooked to perfection.

"I'm glad you liked it."

Gemma nodded. "And we're real glad you were able to join us."

"I appreciate the invitation." John wiped off his hands on his cargo shorts then reached toward Eve.

She took his hand, offering him a contented smile.

When he'd first heard that Eve liked to camp, this right here was what he had imagined. Minus cuddling up under a blanket by the fire. They'd die of heatstroke if they tried that in the middle of June.

Not a day went by that John didn't give thanks for this time with Eve. It'd been two months since the nightmare Jackson Arends put them through. Eve's side had healed nicely, and her nightmares were becoming less frequent.

Getting away from the station and enjoying the peace of the river near Clearwater was exactly what everyone needed.

They'd enjoyed a day of fishing, kayaking, and relaxing. The sun was sinking below the horizon, and the slightly cooler air felt wonderful as it came in off the winding river nearby.

Carlton stood and stretched before reaching out a hand to his wife. Gemma followed suit.

"I think we're going to go for a walk before it gets too dark." She gave Eve a not-so-subtle wink. The older couple wandered up the dirt path together.

John chuckled. "I like your parents."

"I'm glad because they like you, too. A lot." A leaf fell from the tree above them and landed on Eve's sleeveless shirt. She picked it off and dropped it on the ground. "I'm pretty sure they'd adopt you if they weren't already hoping you might join the family in a different capacity."

"I picked up on the hints."

While Eve's parents were a bit more vocal about their thoughts concerning Eve and John's relationship, his parents had thrown in their own fair share of opinions. They'd made it clear Eve was wonderful and that he'd be an idiot if he ever let her go.

He happened to agree with all of them.

Eve gasped and leaned forward in her chair. "Did you see that?" She pointed toward a bush next to her small tent.

John watched the bush for a moment or two. "See what?"

The words were barely out of his mouth when a tiny green light flickered. A moment later, a second and then a third blinked in the same general vicinity.

The glow of the fire made it difficult to see them very well. John stood, still holding Eve's hands, and gently tugged on hers until she joined him. Together, they quietly walked toward the bush where they stood in silence and waited.

It wasn't long before multiple floating lights began to flicker here and there.

Eve leaned into John. "I love watching fireflies. That's partly why we come out here every June. Camping wouldn't be the same without them."

After several moments, she turned to look at him and seemed surprised to find him watching her instead of the fireflies. "What? Do I have marshmallow on my mouth?"

No, but if she did, he'd happily have kissed it away for her.

He shook his head. "I'm just enjoying this moment with you. I've seen fireflies before, but being here with you makes it special. Memorable." John reached into a pocket and pulled out a ring box. He opened the lid, thankful that there was just enough light left in the day for her to see the three stones embedded in an infinity band.

Eve pressed the palm of one hand against her chest. "Oh, John. It's beautiful."

"I want to spend the rest of my life making memories with you. Genevieve Marks, would you do me the tremendous honor of becoming my wife?"

Tears glistened in her eyes as she looked up into his face. "I've never wanted anything more."

John grinned as he placed the ring on her finger, then gathered her into his arms. The fireflies, cricket song, and even the lapping of water in the river faded. All John could hear was the racing of his own heart as he gazed into the beautiful face of his fiancée. "I love you."

She stood on her tiptoes and put her arms around his neck. "I love you, too."

He kissed her with the love he'd kept hidden for far too long. It'd always been there, waiting to be discovered just beneath the surface.

Special Thanks

Steph, Rachel, and Elizabeth, if it weren't for you ladies, I never would have finished this book. I can't thank you three enough for our many brainstorming sessions. You are rock stars.

Melissa, I am so very grateful for our friendship. You've really encouraged me this year. After taking so much time off from writing before 2023, it was hard to jump back in. But you've been there, cheering me on, and it means so much.

Kris and Denny, thank you both for taking the time to read through an early copy of my book. Your insight is always priceless, and you both catch those typos that seem to slip by everyone else.

I wanted to send a special shout-out to my amazing readers who are part of the Readers with Heart team. Thank you for all you do!

Doug, Xander, and Sydney, as always, you three are my heart and my home. I love you!

Most of all, Heavenly Father, thank you for carrying our family through these last few months. Your love never fails.

About the Author

Melanie D. Snitker is a *USA Today* bestselling author who writes inspirational romance and romantic suspense. She and her husband live in Texas with their two children. They share their home with three dogs and two terrariums filled with small critters. In her spare time, Melanie enjoys photography, reading, training her dog, playing video games, and hanging out with family and friends.

https://www.melaniedsnitker.com/

Books by Melanie D. Snitker

Danger in Destiny

Out of the Ashes

Frozen in Jeopardy

Beneath the Surface

Caught in the Crosshairs

Running from the Past

In Pursuit of the Truth

Assigned to Protect

Surviving the Storm

Forged by Fire

Brides of Clearwater

Marrying Mandy

Marrying Raven

Marrying Chrissy

Marrying Bonnie

Marrying Emma

Marrying Noel

Books by Melanie D. Snitker

Love's Compass Complete Series

Finding Peace

Finding Hope

Finding Courage

Finding Faith

Finding Joy

Finding Grace

Love Unexpected Complete Series

Safe In His Arms

Someone to Trust

Starting Anew

Healing Hearts

Calming the Storm

I Still Do

Don't Kiss Me Goodbye

Sage Valley Ranch

Charmed by the Daring Cowboy

Welcome to Romance

Fall Into Romance

A Merry Miracle in Romance